GLADIATOR

BEN ELLIOTT

SCHOOL

ZIPPER BOOKS

GLADIATOR SCHOOL Ben Elliott

Copyright © 2000 Ben Elliott
3 Broadbent Close London N6 5GG. All rights reserved.

First printing June 2000. Printed in Finland by WS Bookwell.
Cover photography © 2000 Prowler Press

web-site: prowler.co.uk
• ISBN 1-873741-52-9

British Library Cataloguing in Publication Data.
A catalogue record for this book is available from the British Library.

CHAPTER 1

In one practised move, Paris swung himself up on the ivy and lay quite still along the top of the wall. He listened hard. A handful of cicadas broke the silence of the April night with their whirring monotone. In the distance, a dog barked. Another mutt, close by, answered. A light breeze ruffled Paris' thick blond hair and brought a faint gust of male laughter from some late night drinking party still further away.

The young man knew, however, that most of the lavish villas that dotted the countryside of fashionable Campania were the summer residences of wealthy citizens of Rome. At this time of year, many were still empty, or guarded by a handful of retainers. In the three months since he had run away from his uncle's home in Genua, far to the north, he had become something of an expert at spotting the dwellings that would provide a few days' free food and shelter - a warm bed of straw in an outhouse, nuts and vegetables filched from their estates.

Paris turned over on his back and stretched, nestling luxuriously in the thick ivy. The warm southern night felt so good on his bare skin after the weeks he had spent trying to find refuge from the icy mists of the north.

He felt a surge of triumph: so far, everything had gone according to plan. As he had long vowed, he had made his escape just after his seventeenth birthday. How he had loathed his life in the house of the uncle who had adopted him after his parents' death. This was a man who clung to the old-fashioned notion of the all-powerful pater familias for whom wife and children were property to treat as he liked. In Paris' case, this meant constant beatings for the slightest misdemeanour.

Paris chuckled at the thought of his uncle's fury once his escape had been discovered. He had even managed to sneak from under his nose the vital documents which proved the boy's status as the son of freed slaves and heir to his father's considerable estate. Paris congratulated himself on having found a hiding place for the scrolls close by, where they would be safe until needed. And that moment should be soon, he thought, for he had almost reached his destination: the estate at Stabiae, just beyond Pompeii, which had been his father's and would now be his. Paris smiled. There was just one person he missed - the sweet slave boy Epaphra with whom he had spent many a blissful night. How the youth had wept when Paris confided the secret of his imminent escape. Yes, he did miss Epaphra and his nightly ministrations. The young man ran his hand over his chest and stroked the growing bulge under his short tunic. No, not yet, he told himself. There were more pressing needs to be met: he had not eaten since early morning.

The boy squinted down into the dark shadows on the other side of the wall. He could make out rows of trees - fruit trees, if he was lucky - and the bulk of a large villa beyond. Paris knew that it was necessary to take especial care with the grander residences which were more likely to be inhabited all year round – sometimes maintained by a large permanent staff of slaves. But this impressive dwelling showed no signs of occupation.

He glanced up. A feathery veil of clouds stretched overhead, marbling the sky with moonlight. A burst of illumination revealed rooftops and columns rising from the trees on the surrounding hills. They were still and ghostly like rich men's tombs. Just as suddenly, a patch of thick cloud threw a blanket of velvet darkness across them.

Seizing the moment, Paris dropped from the wall, causing barely a whisper in the long grass. He paused, staring hard into the darkness through narrowed eyes, straining to catch the sounds of men. Nothing. Just the thin piping of bats, wheeling erratically over the trees like leaves in a wind. With long, low strides, he moved forward, darting swiftly and silently from tree to tree in the direction of the villa.

'Treat me kindly, goddess,' the young man prayed to the moon: 'Keep your face veiled. When I come into my inheritance, I will dedicate a shrine to you and offer daily sacrifice.' To the boy's relief, clouds kept the orchard in shadow.

He reached up into a nearby tree and felt nothing but small hard pears, not yet ready to yield themselves to his grasp. Paris changed direction, skirting the villa, rather than drawing any closer.

He crept along an olive grove, alert as a cat, poised for flight.

Although his body was not yet fully developed, it was already as hard and muscular as a statue of a Greek ephebe. The years of training in the palaestra had paid off. In the past few months, on a diet of nuts, raw vegetables and water, he had shed the last of his puppy fat and his body had begun to mature. His prowess as an athlete had served him well, too. On many occasions he had had to flee from dog and man, shinning up trees and vaulting high walls.

A sharp fragrance pricked his nostrils. 'Apples,' he thought, feeling the saliva spurt painfully under his tongue. He pulled down a branch, inhaling the bittersweet smell. Hungry and thirsty after hours on dusty footpaths, he greedily sank his teeth into one of the hard waxy globes, without even removing it from the branch. He sucked in his cheeks: it was not yet ripe. Yet he had to eat something – even if he would suffer stomach pains later.

Having satisfied his hunger, at least for the moment, Paris settled himself at the foot of the tree and turned his attention to other needs. He ran one hand across his chest, noting with satisfaction the silky down that had begun to sprout in the past few months. Epaphra would surely like that. His other hand strayed under his tunic, gently stroking the hard white pillar which rose from a halo of golden hair. His fingers rotated the silky foreskin, sliding it over his rosy cock-head on a film of love-juice. How many times had Epaphra fondled him in this way while they lay together at night? He smiled contentedly as his thoughts turned to the curly-headed lad.

Paris awoke with a start. His back was stiff and the night had grown chilly. He must have been asleep for some time. He cursed himself for his stupidity. Instinctively, he knew that something had alarmed him - a noise or a movement – quite close. An animal or a bird, he reassured himself. Paris remained motionless, listening. Distinctly, from a few feet away, the sound came again. Something between a sigh and groan. It was human all right, and very familiar - the sound that Epaphra would make when Paris made love to him. He now discerned two dark forms in a clump of trees directly before him, one bent over a low branch, the other upright behind him and thrusting.

At that moment the clouds were torn away, like a veil from the face of the moon. Paris looked up in fright. Their attention drawn by the movement, the faces of the two men in the trees turned towards him. For a moment all three froze in fear and surprise. Then Paris' instincts took over and he was sprinting through the trees, his tattered cloak streaming behind him.

Befuddled by sleep he tried to retrace his steps through the orchard. But he had wandered further than he had realised. Behind him he could hear the voices not just of two but of many men accompanied by the barking of dogs. The cries seemed to be coming from all around him. There were sounds of laughter, too and drunken whoops. It was a midnight hunt and he was the prey.

Out of the corners of his eyes, he could see lanterns moving to head him off. He darted this way and that to confuse his pursuers but the moonlight was now so bright that these manoeuvres were of little use. In his panic, he had lost his bearings and looked around desperately for landmarks.

A blinding blow to his forehead sent Paris reeling on to his back in the grass. Out of blackness, Paris became dimly aware of a ring of flickering lanterns above him. Then he saw faces: a circle of young men, staring curiously down at him, whispering to one another and giggling. They were dressed in fine tunics as though they had been disturbed during a banquet.

The young men fell silent and parted to reveal the rough, weather-beaten face of a middle-aged man. He was panting heavily and his thick black wig was slightly askew. He glanced down at Paris and then looked up. 'Praise to the god,' the man whispered, making a superstitious gesture with his fingers. 'Priapus himself stopped the intruder.' Coming to his senses, Paris realised that he had collided with a bronze statue of the lustful god, glaring down at him from a pedestal, clearly recognisable by his enormous erect phallus. The rampant metal appendage had struck the mighty blow that had stopped the boy in his tracks.

At a word from the man in the wig, the slaves fell on Paris, half-dragging, half-carrying him into the villa. Two brawny young men pushed Paris face-down over a narrow bronze table. They held his arms, stretched full length, while two more roughly splayed his legs apart, grasping his ankles firmly. The others crowded round expectantly. Pinned to the table as he was, Paris could tell that this was the triclinium of a very rich man. Ornate bronze candelabra illuminated lavishly frescoed walls. The table was laid with a half-finished banquet set out on elaborately worked silver and gold vessels. Glinting with gold in the rich mosaic floor below him, he read the motto Lucrum Gaudium: 'Wealth is joy.'

The man in the black wig, which he had now set straight, bustled into the room. Judging by his fine tunic and heavy gold jewellery, this must be the master of the house, Paris thought, or at least a prominent servant. The man paced up and down, running the leather thongs of a whip through his fingers. 'Know, thief, that you have violated the property of the merchant Diogenes - me,' he declared with a pompous little bow.

He spoke Greek with an Alexandrian accent. A former slave who had made a fortune, and showed it off as ostentatiously as possible, thought Paris. He knew the type. His own father had been a freed slave, but a cultured man, from Hellas itself, who had earned his freedom as a tutor to wealthy Romans.

'Now you must pay the price of your villainy, as the law prescribes,' bellowed Diogenes, thrusting the leather handle of the whip under the boy's chin and forcing his head back. 'Let's take a look at you, then,' he said and let out a low gasp. 'Well,' he added appraisingly, 'it's a little blond Alcibiades. A bit dusty, but a regular head-turner, nevertheless. Your name, boy?' When Paris remained sullenly silent, Diogenes jerked the whip-handle hard. 'Your name, slave, before I beat it out of you,' he hissed.

'Paris,' spat out the young man, furious at his impotence. 'And I'm not a slave. I'm a second-generation freedman.' He emphasised these words, knowing that they gave him superior status to Diogenes, despite the older man's blatant wealth.

'Oh, so you're not a slave,' taunted Diogenes, trying, unsuccessfully, to mimic Paris' cultured Greek pronunciation. 'And I'm the Emperor's mother. You face a far more severe punishment as an escaped slave. But first it is my right to exact the penalty for the crime you have committed against my household.'

Diogenes had now moved behind the boy. 'Strip him,' he snapped. First his tattered cloak, then the well-worn tunic were torn from Paris' body. Finally, he felt a pair of hands fumbling between his legs - rather longer than necessary, he thought - as they removed his loincloth.

The young man shivered as Diogenes' rough palm slid lightly down his back, lingering as it passed over his spread buttocks, twin globes hardened by months on the road. It was followed by the leather thongs, lightly trailed. Paris' spine tingled as the tips brushed the tight knot of his anus. He reddened fiercely at being so intimately exposed before so many strangers.

'A shame to damage that lily-white skin with the lash,' mused Diogenes, gently probing between Paris' legs with the whip. 'Yet it seems I would not be the first,' he added, observing the marks left by the many beatings Paris had received from his uncle. 'Clearly your previous masters have had cause to punish you. And I am entitled to exact the lawful penalty.'

As if at a nod from Diogenes, the servants tightened their grip on his wrists and ankles, stretching his arms and legs. There was a collective intake of breath as the slaves moved forward eagerly, eyes widening. Some licked their lips, others whispered. Two kept their distance, Paris noticed. One was a tall handsome lad with long black curls and large dark eyes. The other was just a slender outline in the shadow of a pillar.

Paris waited for the lash to fall. He had received so many beatings in his young life that his back and buttocks were hardened to them. But nothing happened: just silence filled with the crackling of torches, the steady breathing of the servants and a rustle of clothing. Suddenly he felt two firm hands clutch at his waist and then a pain so searing and unexpected that his whole body went limp.

He felt hot breath on his neck and the reek of garlic. 'That's what the law prescribes for household thieves,' rasped Diogenes in Paris' ear. 'You have stolen my fruit, now I will plough your furrow and water it with my seed.' As he spoke, he brutally twisted his cock embedded deep in Paris' tight ass-hole, sending further bolts of pain through the boy's body. Diogenes withdrew his bulky veined weapon as far as the head and plunged it back up to the hilt. The boy grimaced, barely managing to stifle a cry of pain. The slaves drew closer, reaching out to run their hands over his back and through his hair. Some fumbled beneath their clothes while the already erect cocks of others saved them the bother of lifting their tunics.

Grunting noisily, Diogenes began to pump Paris' hole in a steady rhythm. 'The thief...should be sodomised...for his first...offence,' Diogenes panted in time with his thrusts. Paris could feel the man's weighty testicles painfully striking his own like knucklebones shaken in a fist. 'But is it...the first...offence?'

The pain had now subsided as natural lubrication smoothed the strokes of Diogenes' meaty manhood up Paris' back-alley. Pulling out until only the bulbous head was poised in Paris' hole, Diogenes began to slowly rotate it, toying with the boy's sphincter, teasing and stretching it to its fullest capacity. Against the sensitive inner lips of his rectum, Paris could feel the movement of the thick foreskin drawing back and forth across the head with each movement.

As Diogenes slid the full length of his tool back inside him, the initial pain was now replaced by a burning feeling and a strange, not-unpleasant ache which Paris felt mounting behind his balls. 'Perhaps...the little thief... raided...my orchard...before,' moaned Diogenes. He moved his hands to Paris' shoulders allowing him to probe even deeper into the boy's hole, now well-lubricated with Diogenes abundant love juice. 'That merits...further..punishment... pretty one...Lucius!' he called hoarsely. The tall dark young man who up till now had been leaning against a pillar, observing intently, now slowly stood to attention. 'My son...let us administer...the punishment...for multiple...offenders.

Lucius, it appeared, needed little prompting to do his father's bidding. As he crossed the room, he was already stripping off his tunic revealing a stomach and chest of chiselled muscle, a living copy of a statue of Apollo. As he reached Paris, he pulled at the knot of his loincloth and it fell to the floor. Directly in front of his face, Paris saw Lucius' phallus rising straight and proud as a temple column. In the lamplight, he noticed the foreskin drawn blade-tight over the glans which had the purple sheen of a damson. As he watched, a glittering film of viscous liquid spread imperceptibly over the dark head, brimming onto the foreskin, which was slowly retracting.

Paris looked up and his gaze met the deep dark eyes of the young man. Though he appeared to have inherited his father's massive endowment - so it was true what men said about Egyptians! - fortunately, he had not inherited his father's coarse features. The musky aroma of Lucius' cock reached Paris's nostrils, and to his astonishment, he felt his own phallus start to pulsate, rising higher at each beat

Though he was mortified to show such a reaction before so many, he was powerless to restrain it. His lips must have parted as he gazed on Lucius' powerful erection and, before he could stop him, the young man had plunged it deep into his gullet. Though it was long, thick and wood-hard, it slid in and out easily and, far from needing to retch, Paris felt his throat opening wider to receive it. Lucius placed his hands softly but firm-ly on the boy's blond head. Closing his eyes in concentration, he probed ever deeper with his smooth cock-head. Paris could smell the rare orien-tal perfume which anointed the glossy pubic hair, brushing his nose and cheeks.

Now hands were exploring every part of him - his hair, his back, his chest, his legs, tugging on his nipples, alternately pumping or feeding on his erect cock, twisting and pulling on his balls, fingering the places where the manhood of both father and son penetrated deep inside him. The room was filled with the sweet, heavy smell of male arousal. All around him, he could hear laboured breathing and low moans. Above them rose the rau-cous sound of Diogenes whose thrusts now grew faster. Strange, inartic-ulate animal noises accompanied his movements which grew more and more frenzied. Paris felt his whole body shudder as the man slammed into him again and again. The bronze table threatened to buckle beneath him. At the same time, as though he was unaware of all the activity around him, Lucius fucked his mouth with strong slow thrusts.

With a long roar, Diogenes clutched hard on Paris' shoulders, digging into them with his nails, ramming one last time with all the force he could muster. A guttural cry accompanied each long spurt of cum unleashed deep in the boy's guts. Just when Paris was beginning to wonder if Diogenes' huge testes would ever be emptied of their seed, he felt the man slump across his back, almost crushing him with his full weight.

For a moment all movement ceased but for Lucius' long, deliberate strokes. And then, as Diogenes slowly raised his bulk from Paris' body and withdrew his still-hard rod, the boy suddenly realised that his ordeal was far from over. Diogenes had merely declared the festivities open.

The moment that the master of the house had withdrawn his swollen organ, Paris was surrounded by frantic movement as everyone changed places. The slaves holding his wrists and ankles were relieved so that they too could join in the melee, while the others jostled to occupy another cov-eted position.

No sooner had Lucius withdrawn the full length of his prick from Paris' mouth than it was replaced by another. This was shorter but of such girth that his lips were stretched tight around it. It immediately began to roughly hammer the back of Paris' throat. Then the boy felt a warm lean torso against his back.

'Relax, slave. I won't hurt you,' said a soft deep voice which he knew to be that of Lucius, 'Let us both enjoy the worship of Priapus.'

For the second time that night, Paris felt his knees buckle, though this time the cause was not pain but a bolt of sweetness that shot from his bowels to his heart as he felt Lucius' cock sliding slowly into him. He was still dimly aware of the sighs, moans and grunts around him, of the hot breath and purposeful hands of men on every part of his body. But it was as though these were happening far away and to someone else.

All he could think of was Lucius inside him, filling him, making their two bodies one. Sometimes he was aware of the other man's cock sliding smoothly, slowly in and out of his rectum, at others it would batter his vitals with a rough urgency. But both sensations dissolved into a raging glow which enveloped his whole body, torso, head and limbs. At the centre of this glow burned his own hot pole and that of Lucius inside him, although now they had become confused, as though one were the continuation of the other, a single spear piercing and uniting them.

Still thrusting with his hips, Lucius pressed his chest to Paris' back. 'Come now,' the dark young man whispered urgently into the fair boy's ear. 'Come with me.' Up to this moment Lucius had let out nothing louder than a sigh, but now Paris heard a groan which appeared to emanate from deep in the man's belly. He felt it vibrating against the small of his back and rise towards the other man's throat. In response he felt his heart begin to pound and a tingling travel from his hands and feet into his bowels. Lucius let out a long soft moan in Paris' ear as though meant just for him.

Paris felt a cry forced from his own throat as the other man's pole froze rock hard for a moment inside him before it began to buck wildly, spraying his entrails with jets of hot semen. Already almost painfully rigid, Paris' cock responded with spasms of its own, shooting thick arcs of white man-milk onto lips and tongues thirsting to taste the juice of the beautiful blond slave.

Feeling the boy's rectum clutch at his manhood over and over again so intensified Lucius' excitement that he felt a second, even more power-ful orgasm rising inside him. 'Yes,' whispered Lucius in Paris ear, as he spurted fierce streams into the boy for a second time: 'you are mine, slave. All mine. And you always will be.' For a second, both men went limp as a shadow passed over their consciousness.

When Paris finally opened his eyes again, he saw Lucius moving off into darkness, stooping to pick up his discarded tunic and disappear. He was vaguely aware of a thick sweetish liquid dripping from his lips and run-ning down his chin. But before he had time to think, another stiff column was plunged down his throat and he was roughly penetrated from behind once more. As the shaft plunged into his entrails, Paris felt the seed of the last two men squelching out around its root, dripping onto his balls and down the backs of his thighs. A spurt of the warm liquid gurgled out with each new stroke.

By now the slaves were transported in a frenzy of lust. Paris was aware of frantic action all around him. The cheeks of two men were pressed to his own and he could feel their slippery tongues caressing the hairy balls of the man whose rod was pumping his mouth. Something wet was lapping at his own balls. Suddenly he realised that a mouth was greedily slurping the semen that still streamed from his hole. Hot lips clamped on his cock, and, he began to stiffen again, drawn into the mad-ness, the Priapic trance.

Cock after cock gushed a salty flood into his mouth and ass, alter-nating with frantic lips, drinking the liquid from his own mouth or sucking deep draughts from his gaping anus. By the lurid light of the fading lamps, the night became a series of strange visions as Paris watched naked bod-ies knot and weave in a tapestry of ever-changing combinations. Enraged by the reek of lust and the excesses taking place all around them, each man spilled his seed again and again. Paris was aware of the same men taking him with desperate urgency, before and behind, four, five, six times.

Dawn was already casting a chilly light through the curling smoke of the lamps when the last of the young men was sated or rather had dropped with exhaustion. The air was rank with sweat, smoke and semen. The boy's legs were tight with the drying seed of many men. Fresh rivulets still bubbled from the lips of his ass, scarlet and engorged from so much use, trickling down his legs like the waters of a sacred spring.

'The god has been propitiated,' a slurred voice announced and Diogenes lurched into view, his wig now over one ear. Paris realised that he had been watching the entire spectacle, probably from the comfort of a couch and – judging by his appearance – enjoying large amounts of undiluted wine. Diogenes took Paris' chin in his hand. The boy's mouth was caked with a white residue, like that of a child who has drunk deep on a goblet of milk. His eyelids quivered with exhaustion. Diogenes leered down at him. 'Welcome, slave, to the House of Diogenes. Welcome to the Temple of Priapus.'

CHAPTER 2

Paris woke with a strange unfamiliar tune running through his head. The room in which he lay was in semi-darkness: it was small with rough brick walls, probably intended for animals. As it resembled innumerable other outhouses and stables in which Paris had awoken over the past few months, at first he thought he was still free. And then he stirred on his bed of straw and felt the ache between his buttocks. Nightmarish images of the previous night's debaucheries came flooding back. He burned with shame as he recalled the abuse and humiliation.

But there were other memories, too. The feelings that had coursed through his body when Lucius had made love to him. And then, later, when they had done with him and dumped him in this place, he recollected gentle hands that had washed away the discharge of so many phalluses and had applied a soothing ointment. Its sweet smell still lingered. Had that been Lucius, too, he wondered? And that tune? He did not remember music accompanying the revels.

A bolt shot open with a sharp retort and a slab of sunlight fell heavily on Paris' body. For a moment, the boy was blinded by dazzling light. Then he saw a bulky figure blocking the doorway. Paris sat up, squinting into the glare. A burly dark-skinned man stepped into the room.

He had the shaved head of a slave and a purple scar ran down his cheek from temple to chin. The deep furrows which marked his face were belied by the broad, powerful body. 'The master will see you now,' boomed the man. 'I am Pollux, former gladiator of the arena at Pompeii. He has set me to watch over you.' Pollux broke into a slow stupid grin. 'He wants no harm to come to his newly acquired treasure.'

Paris opened his mouth to protest, then thought better of it. He rose and meekly followed the man. The sun was high in the sky and the estate was already teeming with activity. Carts trundled by, stacked high with produce. Lines of slaves carrying agricultural implements snaked grudgingly towards the fields.

As they crossed an ornamental garden, Paris saw the villa, dazzling in the mid-morning sun. Everywhere, servants were at work, pruning, weeding, scrubbing, polishing. In the centre of the garden rose a temple. At each corner crouched a sphinx with a pointed column rising from its back. So Diogenes is a devotee of Isis as well as Priapus, Paris remarked to himself.

They entered the villa through a portico which extended down one side of the complex. Beyond this was a large open courtyard paved with elaborate mosaics. From the exercise equipment that was strewn about, Paris recognised this as a palaestra. It was deserted but for a tall figure, burning incense to a bronze statue of Mercury before commencing his exercises.

Even from behind, Paris recognised Lucius: the long triangle of his dark torso; the buttocks, firm as pomegranates. Sensing their presence, the young man turned. He was naked, but for a leather sweatband that held his glossy black locks from his face. Paris felt his heart skip as he saw Lucius' manhood now hanging limp and heavy between his legs.

The young man fixed Paris with his eyes, a half smile playing on his lips. With his broad shoulders, narrow hips and precisely etched muscles, he resembled an ancient Greek Kouros. He even had one foot planted before the other as if deciding whether to approach or not. In the event he decided not to, instead swinging two heavy weights above his head, the better to show off his rippling torso, glinting with a sheen of sweat. He flashed a dazzling smile.

Pollux led Paris through a bewildering series of corridors. They passed several ornate shrines dedicated to various deities, including a particularly splendid one to the Lares, gods of the household. This Diogenes was clearly a very devout man: perhaps he was not so bad after all.

Finally they entered the master's study. A soothsayer was grubbing among the entrails of a bird, a pheasant, Paris reckoned, which had been sacrificed before a shrine to Mercury. Diogenes' eyes were glued to the bloody organs. He looked up as Paris and Pollux entered.

'We shall continue later,' said the merchant to the soothsayer and crossed to a carved desk set in a large pillared bay. Wooden doors had

Ben Elliott

been folded back so that the room was open to gardens, clearly visible through billowing white curtains of gossamer lightness. Pollux positioned Paris before the desk.

Diogenes slouched in a throne-like chair. He was wearing a different wig today, teased into tight black curls. The man yawned, clearly the worse for wear from the previous night's exertions. He looked lazily up at Paris, planting his elbows heavily on the writing desk, supporting his big ugly head on his fists.

'So, slave, now you have had a chance to sleep on it, are you ready to give up this ridiculous story that you are a freedman?'

'But I am,' insisted Paris angrily, tears of frustration pricking his eyes.

'I must say, you don't look like a slave,' said Diogenes with a crafty chuckle. 'With all that hair. But then, who knows how long it's had to grow back. And that unblemished skin. But what master would reduce your value by branding that beautiful face? So tell me boy, where have you come from?'

'I have travelled from many miles to the north, from the house of my uncle in Genua.'

'You swear to that?' asked Diogenes, narrowing his eyes

'Yes,' replied Paris eagerly, thinking that the man had begun to believe him at last. He searched for an oath strong enough: 'I swear on the tomb of my parents.'

'You are an orphan?' asked Diogenes, a smile playing on his lips.

'My parents were killed in the earthquake of the ninth year of Nero's reign, at their villa near Stabiae, when I was three years old. According to my father's will, my uncle became my guardian and took me to his home in Genua. I am now hoping to claim my father's villa and land which he left to me. It's not far from here.'

'So no one knows you in these parts?'

'Not a soul. I left when I was three.'

'And there is no chance that anyone would search for you here-abouts?'

'None at all. I deliberately left misleading stories of my plans with my uncle's slaves in order to throw him off the scent. Even under torture, he would discover nothing from them.'

'Good, good,' sang Diogenes softly to himself, clapping his hands lightly.

'Now listen,' Diogenes frowned, his voice becoming stern. 'Enough of this nonsense about your uncle and your father. It's plain to see that you're an escaped slave.'

'But I can prove that I'm not.'

'And just how do you mean to do that?' demanded Diogenes.

Paris thought for a moment. He was a prisoner and had no way of retrieving the vital documents. If he were to reveal to Diogenes where the scrolls were hidden, he wouldn't put it past him to destroy them. That would put paid to any hopes of obtaining freedom and claiming his inheritance.

'I'm...not sure,' stammered the boy. 'But I know I could find a way.'

Diogenes rose and began to pace round the curve of pillars behind his desk. 'I have an offer to put to you, a very fair offer, I believe, considering that you are no more than a common thief. Rather than give you up to the authorities as an escaped slave, I will keep you as a slave of my own. You will join the ranks of my favourites and be well fed and well dressed.' While he was speaking, the merchant drew closer to the boy until his eyes were a hand's breadth from Paris'. 'If you are good, you will not be beaten. But I don't want a trouble-maker in my household, so the first sign of rebellion and you're out.' Paris had to repress a shiver. Up close, he noticed for the first time a cold emptiness behind the merchant's eyes – like a man without a soul.

'I can always sell you at the slave market. A pretty young thing like you - clever, too, I'll wager - would be worth the price of a small farm. Especially as your charms have been tested and found to be...considerable.'

Paris thought fast. The authorities would be no more likely to believe his story than this man. If he stayed here, sooner or later, he would have the opportunity to retrieve his documents, or despatch a trustworthy friend to find them. The thought of being at the beck and call of this crude, common trader filled him with rage - especially if last night's humiliations were anything to go by. Why, he was nothing more than a jumped up slave himself. But for the moment the boy could see no alternative than to agree to Diogenes' terms.

As he looked up to give his answer, Paris noticed a familiar silhouette approaching from the garden. The filmy curtain was swept aside to reveal Lucius, now dressed fetchingly in a jewelled belt and a scanty white kilt that barely reached the top of his thighs. His oiled chest and arms gleamed like bronze, veins clearly visible through the taut skin after his recent exercise. Lucius moved behind his father, giving Paris the same half-mocking, half-inviting smile that he had worn earlier. In spite of himself, Paris felt his heart quicken. In Lucius' eyes he read the spark of lust, perhaps more. Suddenly the boy knew he had no choice. 'As you refuse to believe me,' he said aloud, 'then there is nothing I can do but accept your offer. As long as I am in your household, I will abide by our agreement. But, once again, I swear to you on the spirits of my father and mother that I was born a free man and I will be free again.'

'We'll see, we'll see,' said, Diogenes with an odd little giggle. He strode across the room with a surprising burst of energy and consulted an elaborate water-clock. 'It's late and there's much to be done. This afternoon I am due to call on my friend Corax at the gladiator school in Pompeii. And you,' he pointed dramatically at Paris, 'will head my retinue, together with that sweet little dancer, Bion.' Diogenes looked Paris up and down with a frown. 'Take him to the bathhouse, Pollux. Find him something decent to wear. And, in the name of Jupiter, do something about that hair.'

Lucius strolled languidly from the room, shooting a sideways glance at Paris under long lashes. The boy felt the heat of the young man's body as he passed close to him.

'Glaucias, let us get back to work,' called Diogenes to the soothsayer. 'The fleet is due from Alexandria and I wish to consult the stars on the outcome of the journey.'

The villa's private bathhouse was constructed on the same lavish scale as the rest of the complex. White mosaic clouds floated in a blue vault, while on the walls square-sailed ships rode the waves. Strange sea-creatures could be glimpsed through the waters of the tubs.

A team of slaves set to work on Paris, mainly Nubians, the colour of ebony. Two young men oiled and scraped his body. A team of boys cleaned out every orifice with long-practised deftness and a set of brushes in many different sizes. A barber shaved him, trimmed his hair and shaped his golden pubic bush into a neat triangle. Finally, his hair and body were anointed with fragrant oils from the East.

The slave who administered these precious liquids was a slim wiry boy, slightly younger than Paris. He was pale, with dark eyes and a helmet of tight black curls. He carried out his task with delicate skill, almost with reverence. Paris sensed something familiar in his touch.

'Do you like the songs of Alexandria?' he asked Paris, brightly. To tell the truth, Paris preferred the classic songs of Greece to such popular modern ditties, but he did not want to offend the boy and so he nodded. The lad began to sing in the kind of high sweet voice the Egyptians used for such melodies.

The youth's name was Bion, and Paris was not surprised to learn that he had been purchased by Diogenes at the age of ten for his skills as a dancer. As a native of Gades in Hispania, he was an expert in the intricate steps of that region.

As the boy was massaging his legs, Paris suddenly felt a hand slip gently between his buttocks and anoint his still swollen and burning anus with a soothing ointment of a delicious coolness. It had a sweet sharp perfume which Paris recognised. He glanced down at the lad, who smiled back at him with his eyes as he sang. Paris remembered: this was the tune that had been running round his head that morning. It was not Lucius, who had ministered to him after last night's orgy, but Bion.

Despite his youth, it was also the slave's duty to prepare Diogenes' retinue for public occasions such as the trip to the port that afternoon. As he twirled and skipped round Paris, holding brightly coloured tunics up against him to find which suited him best, Bion chatted eagerly, interspersing his conversation with snatches of song.

'Don't judge Diogenes by what happened last night,' he whispered in Paris' ear, so that the other servants could not hear. 'He is a good and generous master, especially to his favourites.'

'That's fine,' Paris hissed back, 'if you are happy to be a slave. But I'm not.'

'Ah, yes,' murmured Bion admiringly as he held up a filmy yellow tunic against Paris' broad shoulders. 'With your blond hair, you can carry that off. Not many of us could.' He slipped the garment over Paris' head, carefully arranging the folds and tying them up with a gold-studded belt. 'We have a good life here,' he went on, in a low voice. 'Diogenes treats his favourites more like sons than slaves. He rewards us well. I already have enough saved to buy my freedom, but I love my life in Diogenes' household and I would not change it.' Bion skipped back to judge the effect of the tunic. He selected a gold headband and, darting behind the other boy, tied back his shoulder-length blond hair.

'Of course, it will take time to get used to the place,' Bion whispered in Paris' ear. 'But I hope you will be happy, as I have been. And remember that you already have one friend here who loves you,' the boy added softly as he carefully arranged Paris' blond curls on his shoulders, leaning back to note the effect. 'Lovely,' he breathed.

The trip to the city turned out to be quite a performance – carefully choreographed by Bion. Diogenes led the party in a gold and scarlet litter, carried by eight Nubian slaves, tall and muscular, black torsos oiled to a shine, naked but for the briefest of scarlet kilts. Wide gold belts and gilded sandals with straps up to the thigh completed their costumes.

Behind, three carts carried Diogenes' prettiest slaves. The journey was over two miles, mainly along country paths and Diogenes did not want his retinue arriving dishevelled and dusty. Bion had seated them carefully so that they would not crease their tunics.

The slave from Gades sat next to Paris in the first cart. 'Ever had a Nubian?' he muttered to Paris, eyeing up the litter-bearers as the cart jolted along the rough track. 'Huge,' he sighed wistfully. During the journey he explained to Paris how this was the most exciting time of the year for Diogenes' favourites. Ever since his wife had died, the merchant moved his household to Pompeii for six months each spring and summer for an endless round of parties and pleasure.

When they were some yards from the walls of Pompeii, the slaves dismounted from the carts and Bion formed them into a procession before and behind the litter. He checked the hair and garments of each slave, arranging a ringlet here and adjusting a fold there.

It was mid-afternoon when Diogenes' party arrived at the port of Pompeii at the mouth of the River Sarnus. Paris and Bion headed the train. The water teemed with small craft arriving and departing with exotic wares. It was market day and customers and traders were still arriving from the surrounding resorts, while others, their boats piled high with produce, bolts of material and brightly painted ceramics, were heading home. Stalls decorated with garlands of flowers had been set up along the docks. Other merchants plied their trade from their boats, throwing pots and garments up to their prospective customers for inspection.

In the midst of all this, Diogenes' fleet of five ships had just arrived from Alexandria and was in the process of mooring and unloading. The noise was deafening. Stall-holders were selling their wares in half-a-dozen languages. Customers haggled vigorously. Garishly dressed courtesans of both sexes called out to the arriving sailors. The women opened their garments with gestures that transcended language, while the boys simply hitched up the backs of their tunics so that their charms were evident to all. Adding to the din were the strange roars of caged beasts that were being carefully winched from the ships' holds and transferred to the dockside.

Arriving in the midst of all this, Diogenes' entourage caused a sensation, which was what he had intended. Paris knew that this part of the country had a reputation for lewdness, but he was taken aback at the coarseness of the comments he heard from both men and women. He flushed scarlet, partly from embarrassment and partly with rage at the fact that he was powerless to react. As a freedman, his instinct would have been to turn on these sailors and tradesmen and reward them with a black eye for their crude remarks. But he was no longer free. He was one of Diogenes' possessions on display. And he knew that these filthy comments were music to Diogenes' ears.

Paris stared hard in front of him so as not to meet any of the lustful gazes which he could feel directed at him from all around. Fortunately Diogenes had brought some of his toughest bodyguards to accompany the procession. For the first time that day, Paris felt reassured by Pollux's bulk plodding stolidly alongside him.

Bion noticed Paris' furious blushes. 'Pompeii is the city of Venus, you know,' he remarked casually. 'Here, love is not afraid to show itself openly. Remarks that would be considered insulting elsewhere are regarded as compliments by Venus' subjects. It does not matter if you are slave or free – people will tell you what they think. And it looks like you've made a good impression,' he grinned, nudging Paris in the ribs.

Paris heard a sudden roar from the crowd behind them and turned to see Lucius speeding along the docks towards them, driving a chariot drawn by two white horse. Those unlucky enough to be caught in its path were forced to leap into the harbour to avoid being trampled under the hooves. To Paris' relief, this latest arrival proved such an attraction that the crowd lost interest in himself and his fellow slaves.

While Diogenes and his son boarded the ships to inspect the cargo and consult the stewards, the slaves were allowed to cool off in the shade of a temporary tavern. They were served draughts of cool water with a dash of wine for flavour. Paris, who was thirsty after the long dusty journey to the city, drained his cup greedily.

At the other end of the trestle at which they were seated, a group of off-duty soldiers were noisily engaged in a game of dice. It was surprising to see gambling taking place so openly, and especially among soldiers - it was, after all, against the law. But it was clear that a free-and-easy atmosphere reigned in these Campanian resorts where it seemed to be a holiday all year round.

'That one down there's looking at you,' muttered Bion from the side of his mouth.

'Which one?' asked Paris.

'The soldier at the end.'

Paris craned his neck to see down the long oak trestle. A soldier, who was not taking part in the game, was staring with a rather solemn expression in Paris' direction and raising his goblet.

'Now he's offering you a drink,' hissed Bion. 'Say, yes: nod or something.'

Paris gave the soldier a tentative smile, not quite sure whether it was wise to encourage the man's advances – especially under the nose of Diogenes and – more to the point – his son.

The soldier called the innkeeper over and spoke to him, gesturing in

Paris' direction. The innkeeper nodded, selected a flagon from a high shelf and filled a large goblet, adding just a dash of water.

He slammed it down on the table in front of Paris. 'A large goblet of the best Vesuvian wine. With the compliments of the military gentleman at the end of the table.'

The soldier raised his goblet once again, this time with a smile that lit up his face.

As Paris returned the gesture, the soldier slid up the bench on the opposite side of the table until he faced the lad. He was lean but firm and muscular, sleek black hair cropped military fashion, eyes dancing with good humour. He reached a powerful forearm across the table to grasp Paris' hand. 'Wine for Ganymede, the cupbearer of the gods,' he joked. 'Or are you Apollo come to earth in the guise of a slave-boy?'

Paris blushed. The man was rather direct – but so warm and charming it was impossible to take offence.

'I am Publius,' the soldier introduced himself. 'A native of the city of Rome. Free born,' he added with a touch of pride. 'I'm stationed here with the Urban Cohorts. The Emperor feels he needs to keep a special eye on this city of rogues. I couldn't forget a face like yours, so I can only assume that you are new here.'

'Yes I am new here,' replied Paris bitterly. 'See those caged beasts that are being unloaded from the ships?'

'Yes,' replied Publius hesitantly.

'Well they are new here too and we have something in common - we are owned by the same man - the merchant Diogenes.'

'I see,' said Publius. 'You certainly don't look or talk like a slave,' he added brightly, taking hold of Paris' hand again. 'So what's your name and who do I need to bribe in order to see you again?'

'My name is Paris-' the boy began, then turned as he felt a heavy hand on his shoulder.

Pollux was standing over him. 'The Master is ready to move on,' he boomed, then made a gesture with his eyes. Paris followed the direction of his gaze and saw Lucius glowering down at the soldier from his chariot.

'I have to go now,' Paris told Publius in a low voice as he scrambled to his feet.

'When can I see you?' whispered the other man.

'Don't try,' said Paris hastily 'It would only make trouble for you and for me.'

Diogenes' entourage now set off again, considerably expanded. Carts loaded with goods, caged animals and birds followed the master's litter accompanied by the procession of slaves. A number of citizens tagged along for good measure, as the caravan made its slow and bumpy way through the gates of Pompeii and along its narrow streets. Publius, now wearing his glittering bronze helmet, walked alongside the party for some way, casually eating an apple and grinning at Paris every now and then.

The Forum was not large but Paris found it beautiful. It was bounded on one side by the shimmering sea and on the other by purple mountains. The shop fronts and the portico of the covered market, already bright with frescos, were festooned with bunting. Down one side of the square was a row of brightly painted statues of local dignitaries. Some plinths did not yet have a statue. 'Diogenes has his eye on one of those for himself,' whispered Bion with a wink.

The company moved at a stately pace around the busy market-place, stopping at each temple to drop off gifts of incense and animals for sacrifice. At the Temple of Venus, Diogenes descended from the litter and was ushered inside by a tall priest in a blue toga.

'Our master is a priest of Venus Pompeiana,' Bion explained, 'like many wealthy merchants in the city. Next year he hopes to be appointed to the Imperial cult in Rome. That's how he makes his contacts in business and politics.'

Lucius took up the rear in his chariot. Every time Paris glanced round, the big dark eyes were fixed on him.

The Temple of Isis rivalled those of the Roman gods in size and splendour. The priests came out to greet Diogenes, sprinkling his party with consecrated water as they tinkled golden sistrums. Diogenes offered them crates of Ibis, a bird sacred to the goddess, which could be found in her temples throughout the Empire.

'Isis is very popular here in Pompeii,' Bion told Paris. 'In fact she is a serious rival to Venus. Isis too is a goddess of love and pleasure: she is known as the corruptress.' Bion's eyes sparkled. 'So we like her. And her secret rites are a bit like one of Diogenes' parties.'

As they walked through the streets, Bion pointed out that a number of houses were painted with large posters recommending Diogenes as aedile for justice in the elections due to take place the following July. Diogenes himself made a great show of pretending not to notice that his name was plastered across the walls of the town.

Paris' heart leapt as he saw a large theatre rising to their right. Like many buildings in the city it was covered in scaffolding. 'A theatre,' he exclaimed. 'I love the theatre – especially the plays of Plautus – and the Greeks.'

'Give me a pantomime with plenty of music and dancing,' Bion retorted. 'You know in some of the new ones, the actors are completely nude?'

Paris looked longingly at the splendid building as they passed it. 'When will it be completed?'

'Soon. It was destroyed in the earthquake of Nero's time. And now it's been restored and enlarged,' said Bion breezily. 'We never go - Diogenes doesn't like the theatre. We're heading somewhere much more exciting,' he added with enthusiasm - 'the gladiator school.' They were now in a narrow alley flanked by high walls. No sunlight penetrated here and Paris felt an ominous chill.

The place did not make the same impression on Bion, however, because he continued to chatter on exuberantly. 'The theatre is fine,' he said. 'But you must admit that there is nothing like the games.' Paris was not prepared to admit anything of the sort, so he just smiled half-heartedly. 'Wait till you see the gladiators,' said Bion with a confiding hand on Paris' arm. 'Just gorgeous – and you know what they say about them don't you?'

'No,' answered Paris blankly.

'Their deadliest weapons are in their loincloths.'

The heavy wooden doors of the school swung open to admit Diogenes and his train. Heavily armed guards barred them securely as soon as the last of the party had entered.

'Wonder if I can get a date with him,' muttered Bion, indicating a fresco depicting Priapus dressed as a gladiator, his member as long and rigid as a cudgel.

They found themselves in a large rectangular courtyard in which burly gladiators were engaged in mock-fights with weapons of wood. It was surrounded on all four sides by a portico. A man marched across the palaestra towards them.

'That's Corax,' hissed Bion, 'The lanista who trains the men. He's an ex-gladiator himself so he knows what he's doing.' Even without this introduction, Paris would have guessed as much. The trainer was probably in his fiftes, but his stocky, muscular build could have been that of a much younger man. Scars on his legs and arms and one across his forehead testified to his fighting past. He wore a full black beard, which probably covered other scars, while his large head was completely shaved. Corax's most striking feature, however, was his fierce glare, the look of a man used to staring death unflinchingly in the eye.

'Welcome, Diogenes,' he grunted. 'News has already reached me from the port that your precious cargo has arrived safely.' The two men withdrew to talk, leaving the slaves to watch the gladiators' drill in the courtyard.

'That is the man who will win the election for our master,' Bion whispered to Paris. 'Diogenes will sponsor a big event in the games next month: there's a boatload of sand for the arena sitting down there in the harbour and hundreds of animals waiting to be killed. Corax will supply the gladiators. No one else in the city could stage such games, and that's how votes are won these days.'

Paris shuddered as he watched the men fight. Though it was called a school and gladiators did indeed train here, the place had the gloomy, oppressive atmosphere of a prison. The courtyard rose two stories on all sides and was hemmed in all round by tall buildings. The blue gloom of late afternoon gave it a strange under-sea feel. He felt himself suffocating, drowning. To be a slave was bad enough, but this was a living death.

There must have been a hundred men practising in the palaestra, their massive torsos bulging with effort and shining with sweat. Paris could identify several different kinds of fighter: Thracians, who employed a dagger and a round shield; retiarii, netmen armed with a net and trident; and myrmillones, Paris' favourites, who fought with the arms of the Gauls. Most of the men sported the shaved head and long side-lock characteristic of the gladiator.

Paris knew that few, if any, of these men were here by choice and few would ever leave. Some were slaves who had been bought for their fighting potential, others were criminals for whom the arena was a slow death sentence. One or two might be the sons of disgraced noblemen. Either way, all were condemned. Yet Paris was surprised to note that this fact did not seem to have dampened their spirits. It certainly did not stop them from noticing the charms of Paris and his companions and shouting out colourful descriptions of what they would like to do to them.

One of the gladiators, a giant of a man with a shaggy fair beard and thick brown hair covering his torso and legs, strode right up to Paris, looked him in the eye and growled like a wild beast. Out of the corner of his eye, Paris saw Lucius reach for his sword. But then Pollux, who had been chatting to a group of his ex-colleagues, placed himself in front of the boy. The gladiator backed away, continuing to stare fixedly at Paris, who, as though mesmerised, could not help but return the look.

'That's Niceros,' Bion whispered to Paris. 'He is the biggest attraction in the arena here in Pompeii - and a big attraction outside the arena, too, for both men and women. They say his endowment would put Priapus himself to shame. As you can see, the loincloth he wears leaves little to the imagination.'

Paris was distracted by voices above him and, glancing up, saw Corax and Diogenes leaning over a balcony on the second storey of the building. They were speaking in hushed tones and both appeared to be looking directly at him. As soon as they saw him watching, however, they moved away from the edge of the balcony and vanished from sight.

As the huge gates swung open again, Paris felt a sense of relief. He could breath again. True, he was a slave, but he was not like those unfortunate men for whom death was the only hope of release.

He longed to emerge from the purple gloom of the high narrow alleyways and into the sunlight.

As they turned a corner, they saw a cart rumbling loudly towards them. Suddenly a loud noise rang out, like a hammer striking an anvil, and the cart stopped short with a strange abruptness. The old cart-horse was wrenched backwards, and almost fell.

Diogenes stuck his head out of the litter. 'What's going on?' he called. 'Get that cart out of the way.'

Two guards of the gladiator school, recognisable from their uniforms, had dismounted from the cart and appeared to be pushing something through the spokes of one of the large wheels.

As they were at the head of Diogenes' retinue, Paris and Bion were closest to the cart.

'Bion, see what's happening,' called Diogenes angrily.

'Come on,' said Bion, grabbing Paris' arm.

As they drew nearer, it was immediately evident what had occurred. The cart had been delivering a batch of slaves, fresh from the market, to the gladiator school. Rather than face his fate, one of the slaves had seized the only route to freedom available to him. He had stuck his head through the spokes of the wheel, which had snapped his neck like a twig. He stared up at Paris through blank, hideously bulging eyes, his distended neck twisted weirdly from his shoulders. The young man felt that he was going to vomit.

That night, unruffled by the incident, Diogenes dined with the same group of favourites that had taken part in the orgy the previous evening. His dirty comments and his manhandling of the slaves lying next to him suggested that tonight's party was heading in the same direction. But before that could happen, Lucius rose to leave and, with a nod to his father, took Paris by the hand and led him from the table. Inevitably, Pollux doggedly followed his charge and stationed himself outside the door of Lucius' chamber.

The instant they were alone, Lucius' strong arms were around Paris, squeezing him painfully. Their open mouths met, tongues exploring furiously. Lucius tore Paris' tunic and loincloth from his body, shedding his own at the same time. The boy was now his. He would possess him body and soul. His gestures demonstrated this in the way they mixed tenderness with a rough urgency. While he ran his fingers gently through Paris' hair, he bit the boy's red lips until he drew blood which he savoured with his tongue.

Lucius forced Paris down on to the hard narrow bed. He ground his

erection hard against that of Paris who experienced both pain and pleasure as he felt the other man's hardness pounding urgently at his
cock and tender balls. Continuing to thrust hard, Lucius began to pull on
Paris' small, immature nipples, rotating them gently at first between thumb
and forefinger, gradually increasing the pressure until the boy winced.

'Show me your pain, sweet boy,' whispered Lucius. 'I want you to surrender to me. From tonight, you will be mine, body and soul.' Paris
groaned as Lucius pulled his nipples away from his body and gave them
a vicious twist. 'Does that hurt?' Lucius asked, staring at the boy with an
expectant smile.

'Yes,' moaned Paris, who felt himself sinking into a mist of pleasure
and pain that he had never known before.

While continuing to play with the boy's tits, Lucius' head sank to
Paris' stiff rod. He nipped at the boy's long white foreskin with his teeth,
before plunging his tongue deep between the silken hood and the head,
running the tip along the groove where prepuce meets shaft. With the
rough flat of his tongue, Lucius caressed the broad upper surface of
Paris's cockhead, causing the boy to whimper with pleasure. To add spice
to his delight, Lucius gave Paris' nipples a vicious tweak. The boy's body
arched in response.

Pushing the foreskin all the way back with his lips, to reveal the
naked glans, Lucius slid his teeth softly over the shiny surface, drawing
another strangled cry from his partner. Slowly, Lucius took Paris' entire
hard phallus into his mouth and rocked his head backwards and forwards
so that the rim of the cockhead clicked softly against the edge of his throat.
At this stage, Lucius' only concern was to tantalise, to torment. He wanted Paris to experience pain as pleasure and pleasure as pain.

Withdrawing his mouth from Paris' rod, Lucius slid his tongue over
the boy's balls and down between his legs. Instinctively, Paris raised his
hips, throwing his legs back against his chest. Lucius' tongue found its
goal, a tight button of flesh fringed by a tangle of soft hair. As he toyed with
the tip of his tongue, he heard Paris sigh and simultaneously felt the button of flesh soften and blossom to reveal moist tenderness.

With unexpected swiftness, Lucius moved his hips to the place his
head had been. Plunging his tongue between Paris' surprised lips, he
forced his rigid manhood with a single rough thrust into the boy's unready

hole. He stifled Paris' cry of pain with a rough kiss.

'Not yet,' the boy protested – 'it hurts too much.' 'I know,' Lucius hissed back, 'stay with the pain, stay with it.' He stared eagerly at Paris' face, as the boy grimaced, raising his head from the pillow. Lucius thrust roughly once again, this time firmly planting his enormous member up to the hilt in Paris' fuckhole. Paris threw his head back in a silent scream, but after a moment's pause, Lucius began to slam vigorously into his still-tight anus, causing him to writhe and clutch at the richly embroidered counterpane.

Paris flushed red with the pain and tears ran from the corners of his eyes. Lucius pumped his ass mercilessly with long hard thrusts, causing the small bed to shake. 'You are mine, Paris... all mine... No one else's... And you always will be,' Lucius panted as he plunged in and out of the boy's vitals.

Lucius clamped his teeth hard on the boy's tongue and dragged his nails down the boy's back. Lost in agonising bliss, the boy gave himself up to Lucius, clutching at the man's torso and returning his violent kisses. Nothing could hold back Lucius' climax. He suddenly pulled his face away from Paris and looked down at the boy with an expression of shock. 'I'm going to fill you with my hot juice,' he exclaimed, and as he did so, he felt the jets painfully and deliberately unleashed into Paris' guts.

Maddened by Lucius' arousal, Paris felt himself tumble over the edge and the seed spilled rhythmically from his own stiff phallus.

For a while, the two men lay silent and spent in each other's arms.

'I've got my father to agree that no one can have you but me,' proclaimed Lucius suddenly, turning a triumphant smile on Paris. 'So we can do this every night, and you will never have to take part in my father's famous parties. I know he'll end up by giving you to me for my own. He always gives me what I want. You'll be mine,' he smiled, caressing Paris' cheek.

'But, I'm yours anyway,' said Paris softly. 'Whatever your father says.' He paused for a second. 'Of course, if I was free, then I would truly be yours - and you would be mine.'

'What do you mean?' asked Lucius with a look of puzzlement.

'I mean that, as I have been trying to tell your father, I am a freedman, and I have the documents to prove it.' He paused for a moment and stared hard at the other man. 'Do you really love me Lucius? Enough to help me win my freedom?'

'Not if that means losing you,' replied Lucius hesitantly, moving his body away slightly.

'Of course you won't lose me. On the contrary, only then can you be sure that you really possess me - because I want to be possessed. As long as you own me simply as a slave, I will never really be yours.'

'So what are you asking of me?' asked Lucius, uncertainly.

'A few days ago, I hid the scroll, bearing the mark of the Emperor Nero, granting my father his freedom. With it is my father's will, leaving all his wealth and property to me. '

'So where are these documents?' asked Lucius cautiously.

Paris smiled mysteriously. 'I hid them in a place where even thieves dare not look - in the sanctuary of the Sybil at Cumae. I went to ask her what my future held and decided that her sacred cave would be the perfect hiding place. If you listen carefully, I will tell you where to look.'

'Were you listening to any of that?' Paris asked as he finished his careful instructions. Lucius smiled and nodded, even though throughout Paris' explanation, he had seemed to show more of an interest in the boy's erect penis than in his words.

'So are you going to help me, Lucius?' appealed Paris. 'There's no one else that I can trust. Then we can love as equals.'

'Perhaps I will and perhaps I won't,' said Lucius with a mocking smile. 'First I need you to prove that you really love me whether as slave or free.'

Lucius took Paris' head between his hands and kissed him fiercely. He pushed down on the boy's shoulders until his head reached the level of Lucius' groin. At the same time, Lucius lifted his hips and pressed the back of Paris' head with his cupped palm, forcing the boy's mouth against his asshole.

Although he had never tasted another man's anus before, Paris found it surprisingly fragrant, the skin soft and silken under his tongue.

Lucius hips bucked and writhed with pleasure. At first, Paris examined the area with tentative licks, discovering a pattern of mysterious crevices and smooth expanses, surrounded by a border of short crisp hair.

This previously forbidden region suddenly expanded into a fascinating miniature world to be thoroughly explored.

The taste and smell of this most intimate part of Lucius' body inflamed Paris with desire. He probed at the puckered skin with his tongue and felt the other man's sphincter slowly yielding to admit it. He felt a glow of pleasure as the slippery, satiny lining of Lucius' rectum revealed itself to his tongue-tip, like a cave of treasures.

So as to be able to thrust deeper, Paris clutched for resistance at Lucius' slender hips. He could feel the sharp outline of the hipbones sur-rounded by taut muscle. Maddened by the sensation in his rectum, Lucius began to thrust and circle with his hips, rubbing his open hole against Paris' salivating mouth, forcing the boy's tongue to probe deeper. Reaching his fingers into Lucius' relaxed opening, Paris eased the grooved channel apart so that his tongue could penetrate still further into the dark, musky depths. A long moan escaped from the other man's lips.

Glancing up, Paris noticed Lucius' pole rearing and jerking from the stimulation to his asshole. Beyond the cock, he could see his lover's face, eyes closed, lips wet and parted.

Roughly, Paris pulled the rigid member towards him and began alter-nately to suck the purple, swollen cockhead and poke his rigid tongue into the engorged lips of Lucius' hole. The other man's groans increased in vol-ume and the thrusting of his hips became more urgent.

Raising his head, Paris slid the whole bulk of Lucius' manhood down his throat in one swift move. At the same time, he pressed two fingers deep into his anal canal. With circling movements of his head, Paris manipulated Lucius' rigid glans against the back of his throat. He could feel the hard walnut of Lucius' prostate become ever more rigid as he massaged it with his finger-tips.

'Feed on my cock. Drink my man-milk,' Lucius groaned. 'Let me feel your throat,' he urged, pressing his pubic bush against Paris' mouth.

'Feed on me, Paris. Drink my milk. Drink every drop,' he moaned.

Lucius' prostate clenched, rock-hard. He began to shoot. At first Paris could feel the pulse against his lips at the root of Lucius shaft. Quickly, he pulled his head back till his mouth was halfway down the rigid meat, and made fluttering movements with his tongue just under the cock-head so that he could feel and taste the sweet jets of Lucius' ejaculate bathing his taste-buds over and over. Lucius' moans of pleasure increased at the extra stimulation until finally his body collapsed on the bed, motionless with exhaustion.

'You don't have much respect for your father, do you,' Paris commented, as he nestled against his lover's shoulder.

'I think he's a fool. Which is good in a way, because I manage to get everything I want out of him. He built me the palaestra where you saw me exercising this morning. And then there was the chariot I was driving today. He pays for me to attend the school for Knights in Pompeii, which is only open to the sons of wealthy men.'

'I'll say one thing for him: he is a very religious man. I have never seen shrines to so many gods in one house.'

'He's a very superstitious man – and rightly so,' responded Lucius. 'He's been luckier than any man deserves to be. He went from slave – a sailor on the Alexandria route – to wealthy merchant and freedman in just a few years. Then he married into the Roman aristocracy – what my mother saw in him I'll never know – and inherited a huge fortune. All with little effort and even less brain. So, to guarantee continued good fortune, he offers sacrifice to every god he's heard of – bar the god of the Jews, because then he'd have to give up all the rest.'

'Which of the gods is he most devoted to?'

'Mercury, I'd say.'

'The god of trade and the sea.'

'And of thieves,' sniggered Lucius.

For the two young men there was only one deity that night. It seemed that Venus of Pompeii had granted them the power to celebrate their love as many times as they wished, far more than would normally be possible even for young men as potent and aroused as they were.

'Let us pledge ourselves to one another by mingling the sacred juices of love, the milk of Venus,' whispered Lucius. He sat astride Paris' body, and placed the slit of his hard member against Paris' slit, as though the two small glistening mouths were clamped in a kiss. Wrapping his fist

Ben Elliott

around their foreskins, he began to manipulate them backwards and forwards so that one man's foreskin alternately grazed his own and then the
other man's cock-head.

As Paris felt his glans stimulated first by his own foreskin and then by
his lover's, the sense of intimacy was overwhelming. The head of his penis
was like a burning coal that grew hotter and brighter with the friction of the
silken foreskins until it reached an unendurable intensity.

They came together, the two white jets bursting forth at the same
instant, two torrents fighting against one another, bathing the other's cockhead with each hot fresh spurt, filling each other's foreskins with a sacred
intermingling. After that, neither man could bear to have his member
touched for several minutes.

Paris and Lucius spent that night sharing their bodies and their
thoughts. The more they discovered, the more their curiosity was stimulated. When dawn glowed pink over the mountains in the east, their
hunger had not yet been satisfied.

CHAPTER 3

Over the next few weeks, the evenings followed the same pattern: the two lovers would dine at Diogenes' table and then withdraw to Lucius' chamber where they would make love half the night.

'How is it that you do not have a single hair on your chest and legs?' asked Paris, running his hand over the ridges of his lover's abdomen after a particularly energetic bout of coupling.

'Because Bion removes them with a mixture of hot oils from the East,' giggled Lucius. 'That way the muscles show better – like a marble statue's.'

'Much as I adore you,' smiled Paris, 'I think you are a spoiled brat. You always get what you want and that isn't good for you.' At the back of his mind was the fact that Lucius still had not responded to his request to retrieve the documents that would prove he was a freedman.

Paris was convinced that Lucius believed his story, but it was also clear that Lucius was happier to have him as a slave than run the risk of giving him back his freedom.

'So what?' said Lucius, slipping his arms around Paris and pulling him down on to his chest. 'I'm no different to any of my friends. Their fathers indulge them, too. There's no harm in it.'

Paris frowned. 'My uncle brought me up the old-fashioned way: he never gave me anything but floggings. Strange as it may seem, I now find I'm almost grateful. At least it gave me the determination to find my own way. Of course, I didn't expect things to turn out like this. But I know I will win my freedom back one day. And if a thing's not worth fighting for, it's not worth having.'

'That's enough philosophy for one night, my little Socrates,' said Lucius. 'You know I hate such gloomy talk. Let's get back to some serious business. Now what's this?' he exclaimed in mock surprise, clutching Paris' member which, as always, had quickly revived after their first round of love-making.

'You don't take me seriously, but one day you'll remember my words,' said Paris. His lover did not notice the fleeting look of sadness that passed across the lad's features.

Paris was not sure if Diogenes approved of his son's infatuation. But it certainly suited their purpose that he had other matters on his mind at the moment. The month of May was a busy one in the arena at Pompeii, and Diogenes had chosen the last few dates in the calendar to stage a series of spectacular events featuring the animals he had imported from Egypt, as well as Corax's star gladiators. To fight the beasts, the finest bestiarii had been brought down from the Bestiarius School in Rome, where gladiators were taught the special techniques needed for animal combat. 'Up with Niceros the valiant gladiator,' proclaimed the posters. 'Up with the munificent Diogenes, sponsor of the games, who is running for aedile in the next elections.'

As editor, Diogenes, in a chariot drawn by four horses, headed the procession round the arena which marked the start of each day's games, acknowledging the applause of the crowd with gracious waves and little bows, no doubt mentally translating the din into numbers of votes.

A special ringside box was provided for the editor and his household. Lucius made sure that Paris was always seated next to him and would often ostentatiously hold his lover's hand and steal kisses during the games, even though they were in full view of the crowd. It was up to Diogenes, as editor, to decide on the fate of vanquished gladiators. Corax's men were always spared. But to others, he rarely showed mercy.

The Pompeiians were proud of the fact that their town boasted the first stone arena to be built in the Empire. It could accommodate 20,000 spectators and was usually packed not only with locals but with visitors from nearby towns, drawn by the names of famous gladiators trained at the renowned school of Capua. Some years earlier there had been riots in the amphitheatre, resulting in many deaths. Now the games were always patrolled by troops. To Lucius' annoyance, Publius was assigned sentry duty at the entrance to their box and would take the opportunity to smile and bow to Paris each time they entered and exited.

At the conclusion of the games, Diogenes threw a lavish banquet for Corax and his gladiators at the villa. The merchant had spent weeks supervising the preparations and was determined that the details should remain shrouded in mystery until the night. Not even Lucius had any idea what was to happen.

Diogenes knew that his favourites were incapable of keeping a secret, so he had a team of slaves brought down from his villa in Rome to work on the elaborate arrangements. Special quarters were set up for them in disused outhouses on the edge of the estate and they were not allowed to mingle with the other servants.

Diogenes had chosen a pavilion in the grounds of the villa as the setting for the banquet. It was out-of-bounds to all but the team in charge of the organisation. But it was clear from the frequent delivery of paints and building materials that the edifice was being completely remodelled to provide a unique setting for the festivities.

Despite all these precautions, gossip and speculation about the plans for the evening were rife in the merchant's household. Bion, who was in charge of costumes, gave excited daily reports to Paris. Diogenes had sent scouts to his various estates throughout the Empire, even as far as Alexandria, to select the most beautiful among his male slaves who would provide the entertainment, and serve at the feast.

The merchant had often boasted that he had no idea how many slaves he owned - he had personally seen maybe only a tenth of them - and anyway scores were being born each day. For the first time, the finest male specimens of his vast staff would be brought together in one place. It was said that the choice would include the most handsome sailors from Diogenes' fleet of merchant ships. This caused great excitement amongst the slaves, as sailors were prized for their beauty and sexual prowess.

Sure enough, the new slaves began to arrive at the port of Pompeii. As each new shipment was delivered, Bion gave detailed reports to Paris and the other favourites, informing them who among the newcomers was the most beautiful, the most muscular, the most splendidly endowed.

In the final days before the feast, the gossip among Diogenes' favourites reached fever pitch, as they speculated wildly on the form of the evening's entertainment. Although they had been kept completely in the dark, they had been assured that they would be in attendance. Knowing their master's predilections, they had a good idea of the general direction the party might take and the knowledge that both gladiators and the stable of gorgeous new slaves would be involved drove them into a frenzy of anticipation.

On the day of the banquet, the resident favourites, including Paris, were brought to the Pavilion well before the guests were due to arrive. Together with a large crowd of the new slaves, they had already spent several hours at the baths, where they had been cleaned, depilated, shaved and perfumed. There, seeing the new arrivals stripped naked, Paris realised that Bion had not exaggerated their charms. The size of their members had undoubtedly been a factor in their selection. They were all above average in that department and some of them were so impressively endowed that they would have attracted a crowd in any public bathhouse.

A large dressing room had been provided in the Pavilion. Rows of costumes were hanging from hooks and the slaves were standing around naked for some time while Bion and his team of dressers carried out their work. It was not yet clear what the theme of the evening's celebrations was to be, but it seemed to Paris that the outfits were elaborate variations on the clothes worn by shepherd boys, complete with a sling for carrying lambs.

Rather than being made of rough wool and sheepskin, however, they were gossamer confections of the finest silk, in a dazzling array of different colours and patterns, embroidered in silver and gold and sewn with semi-precious stones. Though there must have been a hundred slaves gathered in the dressing room, Paris could not see a single costume that matched another in colour or detail. Glancing around him as he donned his tunic, he realised that the lower part of each of the garments was made from material as soft and thin as a cobweb so that the wearers' penis and buttocks were in full view.

Bion directed this operation and it took several hours before all the young men had been fitted and checked. As a final touch, crowns of wild flowers were brought into the dressing room and placed on the heads of each of the slaves at the last minute so that they would be fresh for the arrival of the guests. Beautiful and fragrant as a garland of flowers themselves, the youths were led to their places in the new banqueting hall and assigned to couches arranged round tables scattered throughout the large room.

As Paris glanced about him, he was left in no doubt as to the priapic theme of the evening. A team of artists had decorated the walls with frescos depicting the loves of the gods for young men - Jupiter and Ganymede, Hercules and Iolaus, Apollo and Hyacinth. Their huge erect members were painted so realistically that they appeared to protrude from the walls. In the case of the representation of Jupiter, his massive appendage was in fact a piece of sculpture which extended a good five feet into the room. The carved phallus had been designed as a fountain which sent a never-ending stream of divine semen cascading into a pool in the centre of the dining area.

Light was provided by large free-standing brass candelabra. Paris noted that the many branches curving out from the top of each of these took the form of huge erect phalluses. Indeed, the main stem of the candelabrum was a colossal erection, complete with bulging testicles which provided the solid base on which it stood. Tintinnabula, in the form of bronze erections decorated with tiny bells, were suspended from the roof of the hall, constantly sending up their tinkling prayers to Priapus.

Paris began to feel uneasy about the role that he and the other slaves would be expected to play in the forthcoming revels. He wondered if Lucius had had any advance warning of Diogenes' plans. Certainly, his lover had sworn that he had no idea what his father was planning - just that it was to be the most spectacular party the ambitious merchant had ever thrown.

As these thoughts passed through his mind, a band of musicians took their places next to an ornate entrance at the far end of the chamber. Six horn players raised their huge curved instruments and blared out a raucous fanfare of the kind normally reserved for the arena or the circus. Usually such horns were designed to look like fish, but Paris was astonished to realise that these had been fashioned as coiled phalluses - another of Diogenes' extravagances.

The curtains covering the wide doorway were whisked apart and, in a solemn procession, the gladiators entered, led by Diogenes and Corax. Paris was surprised to see that Lucius, looking somewhat bemused, accompanied them.

A number of slaves had been chosen to show the guests to their places. There must have been a hundred gladiators in all, Paris guessed: they were finely dressed, probably in robes provided by Diogenes. Paris was surprised to see them so subdued. They were on their best behaviour - for the moment at least.

Lucius passed close to Paris on his way to his place at the top table between his father and Corax. Paris saw his lover half-turn towards him with a puzzled frown and for a moment it seemed as though he were about to speak, but then he looked away and moved on.

Paris felt a hairy arm jostling roughly against his own as one of the gladiators lay down on the couch beside him. Turning, he found himself staring into the large grinning countenance of Niceros.

As the last of the gladiators took their places, the fanfares concluded and the band struck up a beguiling melody on harps and flutes. Several curtained doorways behind the diners opened up to admit a procession of naked slaves, their bodies oiled and glistening, each bearing a silver bowl. None of these faces were familiar to him so Paris assumed that the lads were part of the new shipment from abroad.

Although they were all beautiful of face and body, their skin-shades varied from alabaster white to date-brown. Some were blond, others brown-haired and a few had sleek blue-black locks. Some wore curly tresses while others had hair that hung straight in a smooth curtain. But what they all had in common was a luxuriant mane that cascaded to their shoulders. Carefully rehearsed, each young man moved quickly to his assigned place, kneeling with bowed head next to a guest.

They were rapidly followed by dancing boys dressed in long transparent robes, leading columns of naked serving-lads carrying the first delicacies of the evening. The opening formalities over, the hall teemed with activity, resounding with conversation and laughter. The gladiators eagerly raised phallus-shaped goblets of coloured glass to slaves who served them with wine from silver flagons.

They roared with delight as the first dish was placed before them. Setting the tone of the evening, it consisted of asparagus tips and quails' eggs arranged to look like erect penises, complete with pairs of testicles. These were followed by a bewildering array of confections, on the same theme, which were piled high on the tables between the couches.

Paris noted with some disgust the gladiators' complete lack of table manners - hardly surprising, he thought, as most of them were the scum of the earth. Glancing in Lucius' direction, curious to discover his lover's reaction to the proceedings, he suddenly realised the purpose of the long-haired slaves.

Ostentatiously, Diogenes held up his fingers, greasy with sauce and gravy, dipped them in a silver water bowl held by the kneeling slave and then wiped them on the boy's long, blond curls. As soon as they noticed this, the gladiators followed suit, braying with laughter, pulling so roughly on the hair of the slaves that some winced and even shed tears, though they did not utter a cry or move from their crouching positions.

Diogenes had provided a rare vintage of Falernian wine for the feast. Although diluted with water, as was customary at all but the most dissolute parties, it was still very strong and the gladiators soon became rowdy. The phallic designs of many of the dishes were awakening other appetites.

The crowning glory of the feast was a vast circular cake with large pastry erections jutting from its sides. A fanfare on the horns greeted its entrance. At a signal from Diogenes, the chef pressed a plunger in the centre of the cake which caused the 'phalluses' to ejaculate enormous jets of thick white custard. The guests were so surprised and delighted that they burst into applause.

While slaves served each gladiator with his own pastry phallus, some were already finding other uses for the beautiful lads whom Diogenes had supplied as human napkins. Roaring with laughter, they grabbed their slaves by their hair and forced them down on their erect cocks, while others pressed the faces of their slaves between their ass-cheeks.

The lusts of the gladiators were further inflamed by the entertainment Diogenes had provided while they ate. Naked dancers executed patterns of spectacular leaps and lascivious movements around the diners, to the rhythm of castanets. Bion was among these, and his watchful gaze showed that he had been responsible for drilling the others. The nature of the dance was such that, by the end, the performers themselves sported erections and the climax came as they screwed one another onstage. They withdrew just before they ejaculated as proof to the guests that their actions were not faked.

A series of mimes followed, based on the themes depicted in the frescoes - the rape of young men by divine beings. Once again the absolute realism of the rape scenes was beyond question.

The actors playing the gods were strapping lads, all of them new faces to Paris. They looked impressive: completely nude, muscles glimmering under a coat of metallic paint which covered their faces and bodies - one silver, one gold, one copper, another bronze. These divine creatures had been selected not only for their masculine beauty, but for their phalluses which rapidly swelled to their full impressive stature in the course of the action.

The slaves playing the mortals, on the other hand, were pretty young things, all known to Paris. When the moment of rape came, it was so realistic - shockingly so - that even the gladiators who were at various stages of ravishing their own personal slaves stopped and watched openmouthed. Such struggles and screams of shock and pain could not be faked. Paris - and indeed the whole assembly - were convinced that the slaves playing the mortals had been taken completely by surprise and were not acting at all.

Diogenes roared with laughter and slapped his thighs at the reactions of both actors and audience. It was obvious what had happened. The actors playing the mortals had been tricked during rehearsals into imagining that the rape would be faked, while those performing as gods had been instructed to genuinely violate their partners on the night. Two of the 'mortals' had fainted with the pain and, during the tumultuous applause at the conclusion of the mime were hurriedly carried off by stagehands. As one of these lads was whisked past Paris, he could see the blood still running in rivulets from his violated anus.

Niceros had grunted with pleasure throughout the mime. This was doubtless - at least in part - because he had the head of his slave firmly wedged in his crotch. Although Paris could not quite see what was happening, he guessed from the gagging sounds coming from under the slave's long chestnut tresses that he was having some trouble swallowing Niceros' member.

The gladiator had grabbed at Paris' buttocks a number of times, but the boy had always managed to roll beyond his grasp. On one of these occasions, Paris glanced across towards Lucius who lay on the couch next to his father, to find him glaring back, flushed with annoyance.

At this high-point in the proceedings, Diogenes stood up and slowly led the procession of gladiators from the chamber. Lucius walked alongside his father, and, once again seemed to be about to stop and speak to Paris as he passed. This time, however, Diogenes' face took on a steely expression, his eyes fixed in front of him. He grasped his son by the wrist and steered him firmly forward. The long-haired slaves were rushed out through another entrance. The supper was over. Now the main entertainment was about to begin.

Paris and the other slaves who had remained behind in the banqueting hall were formed into lines and led down a long corridor to what appeared to be another cavernous chamber. In fact they were in the open air. A large rectangular space had been bounded by long friezes painted on canvas. They were on a pastoral theme, depicting rolling hills dotted with villas and temples. The night sky stretched overhead, a pitch-black ceiling sprinkled with stars.

The ground of the enclosure had been landscaped with small hills, caves and streams, and thickly planted with bushes and trees. Light was provided by torches set on the poles holding up the canvas friezes and on pillars dotted throughout the picturesque landscape. Guards armed with spears were stationed along the sides to prevent anyone from escaping under the canvas.

Disoriented, Paris, together with the other slaves, wandered into the strange theatrical setting. At the back of his mind, a small voice was comparing the woodland scene to something he knew well, something he could not place in the confusion of the moment. A sudden blare of horns - this was strangely familiar too - caused the slaves to turn to the opening in the canvas where they had just entered.

The dark shapes of strange creatures slowly began to fill the gap. For a moment Paris thought he was dreaming or hallucinating. Perhaps they had not put sufficient water in the wine at the feast – or maybe they had slipped a herbal potion into the goblets. The dark forms that were now streaming into the fake woodland were not human. Crooked horns sprouted from their brows. Their shanks were broad and hairy. And those grotesque members that hung low between their legs could surely not be human organs.

Among these strange figures appeared one that Paris seemed to know. It too had hairy haunches and horns on its head, but the erect phallus that bobbed grotesquely between its legs was of painted wood. Paris had seen many like it at the Floralia festival each spring.   The creature's face was unmistakable, however. Even under a long wig and fake beard, Paris would have recognised the bloodshot eyes and bloated features anywhere. Diogenes, as the master of ceremonies, was playing Priapus, leading the revels. The gladiators were satyrs, his bawdy attendants.

How appropriate, thought Paris grimly. Satyrs were half-man, half-beast, given to raping human beings of either sex in order to slake their insatiable lust. The description fitted the gladiators perfectly.

There was one difference between Diogenes' costume and those of his followers, however. The gladiators moved into the light and Paris realised that the dark shapes dangling between their legs were arching to life as they eyed the beautiful slave boys that had been provided for their sport. The horns and hairy leggings were costumes: the phalluses were real.

In a flash, Paris realised why the surroundings looked so familiar – they were modelled on the forest glades constructed in the arena to add interest to the staging of wild beast hunts.

A painted temple had been folded back and the long-haired slaves – having been cleaned up after the banquet - were being bundled into the forest scene. Bion and his team of assistants were hastily adjusting skins of beasts which had been strapped to their backs, though, apart from these, the slaves were still naked.

At last it dawned on Paris what was happening. Animals, shepherd boys: these were the traditional rape-victims of satyrs. The gladiators were the hunters and the slaves were their prey. Capture and conquest was to be rendered more piquant by the chase.

The horns rang out again, and this time Paris could place the sound immediately. It was a traditional hunting call – the signal for the slaves to flee for their lives and for the gladiators to give pursuit.

Paris froze as his eyes locked with the fierce stare of one of the satyrs, a hairy colossus who was rapidly bearing down on him. The young man knew those eyes, even before they were accompanied by a low growl. It was Niceros the gladiator, laying claim to his prize. In one hand, he held the net used to trap a man in the arena.

At that moment, Paris' attention was caught by something huge and dark jutting from between Niceros fur-clad thighs. It stood out, large and menacing as a forearm ending in a clenched fist. Though it had the shape of a phallus, it did not seem to be made of flesh and blood. Surely it was carved from wood or fashioned in leather. Its colours were strange and inhuman: the head purple-black, the texture of pumice stone; the veiny column, brown like a gnarled oak-branch.

But the unmistakable throbbing motion of the swollen organ showed that it was indeed a living thing. It resembled the member of an animal – a stallion or an elephant – more than that of a human being. With a feeling of dread, Paris knew that the massive organ aimed squarely at him would not subside until it had fulfilled its savage purpose.

Niceros was almost upon him when movement returned to Paris' limbs. He ducked to avoid the gladiator's hairy paw. Perhaps the youth was not as strong as his huge opponent and, in this make-believe forest, he would inevitably be cornered. But Paris felt sure he could out-run the other man and he was not about to yield without a contest.

Many a chase through an orchard or vegetable patch over the past few months had given Paris the necessary practice to dodge the hills, streams, boulders and foliage that dotted the fake forest. It was clear that - as in the arena - these had been designed partly as obstacles and partly to provide hiding places, thus adding spice to the chase.

As he dodged around bushes and bounded over streams, Paris could see bodies going down all around him. He recognised many of Diogenes' favourites. As they had spent the past few weeks talking about nothing else but the prowess of the gladiators, it was not surprising that they were only too eager to succumb as quickly as possible. They faked resistance very prettily but, Paris felt, fooled no one.

On the other hand, he could see that the newer slaves, particularly the long-haired beauties in their animal skins, were genuinely panicked. He almost collided with one as he leapt over the brow of a low hill and for a moment caught a glimpse of horrified brown eyes under the horns of a gazelle.

The idyllic woodland was now a scene of chaos. It was almost impossible to avoid the figures - animals, shepherds and satyrs - weaving in and out of the artificial obstacles. Already many gladiator-satyrs had descended on their prey who were in various stages of ravishment.

Paris was heading towards a low fence with a rustic stile built into it. He calculated that he could hurdle the barrier without breaking his stride, but as he prepared to spring, his foot slipped on the freshly laid turf and he went sprawling. The fence hit the lad squarely in the chest, winding him. At that moment, with a whistling of weights, Niceros net' folded heavily around Paris' limbs. It was followed an instant later by the crushing weight of the man's body on top of him, roughly fumbling with his legs and arms.

Just as quickly, the pressure was removed and the net was skilfully peeled back. Yet Paris could not move and he realised to his horror that in the few seconds that he had been trapped under the net, the gladiator had managed to lash his wrists with leather thongs to the fence on either side of the stile, while his knees and ankles had been secured underneath it. The crossbar of the stile was wedged between his knees and his buttocks were perched, spread and vulnerable, at the end of the stile, facing Niceros.

Paris tried to turn, but his arms were spread wide, allowing him very little movement. Although, for a few seconds, nothing happened, he could sense the vast bulk of the gladiator behind him and knew that he was preparing that vast inhuman weapon for attack.

All around him, Paris could hear the cries and moans of hunters and hunted - some of these were expressions of pleasure, but he could also detect shrill notes of pain and distress rising above the general din.

Paris felt Niceros' huge rough paws descend heavily on his shoulders and heard the man's laboured grunts as a soft, blunt beating began against his exposed anus. The blows felt curiously harmless and ineffectual, as though from a padded club. But then he remembered how menacing the fist-like member had looked when he had first seen it earlier, protruding obscenely between Niceros' furry haunches.

The soft blows ceased. Pressure was focused on one spot and grew stronger. Paris heard a low growl start deep in the gladiator's belly as he threw the full weight of his mighty frame behind his rigid column. Paris breathed deeply. Niceros had trussed his limbs so firmly that he was unable to move an inch. He was powerless to resist. The only hope of lessening the agony to come was to yield as far as he could to the assault.

As he tried to relax his sphnicter, the boy could feel Niceros' rock-like cockhead stretch the tender skin till it seemed it would tear like papyrus. The gladiator paused for a moment and Paris heard him roughly clear his throat, drawing the saliva together in his mouth before aiming a glob of it just at the point where his glans was half-wedged into the boy's rectum.

Emitting the blood-curdling war-cry he usually employed when dealing the death-blow to an opponent in the ring, Niceros lunged into the lad with the full force of his colossal physique. As Paris blacked out for a moment, he was aware, far off in the distance, of a high-pitched scream, like the cry of a woman in childbirth. When he slowly awoke to the tearing pain that seemed to split his body in two, he realised that the scream had been his own.

The agony gradually subsided and Paris became aware of a fullness in his bowels as though he desperately needed to shit. That massive bulk, he realised, was Niceros' member. Having managed to penetrate the boy's ass with a single vicious stroke, the gladiator had paused for a moment. Now he began to explore the young man's rectum with his club of flesh. Paris groaned as each tiny movement sent out new bolts of pain. For the shaggy gladiator, the knowledge that he was causing such torment acted as an aphrodisiac - though his insatiable lust hardly needed further stimulation.

Niceros employed his unwieldy member not as an instrument of love but exactly as he used the stubby, lethal sword with which he was armed in the arena - as an implement of butchery. He did not care how much he tore at the other man's flesh or bruised his internal organs. He was concerned only with his own satisfaction. Inflamed by Paris' reactions, he clung to the boy's shoulders and began to pump his fuckhole, slamming his wiry black pubic bush against the swollen ass-lips.

The assault on his body had left Paris stunned as though he had been drugged by a witch's potion or the fumes of the oracles' cave in Delphi. Although he had been fucked before, he had never felt such a loss of control in his bowels, the sensation of being totally overpowered.

The feelings in his lower body had released some hidden humour which had affected and intoxicated his senses. Every tiny physical sensation was magnified: the roughness of Niceros' rock-like glans as it twisted in his guts, the awareness of each knotted vein on the tree-trunk shaft as it hammered against his intestines. At the same time he began to be aware that the pain had subsided to a dull ache and that the ache was melting into a glow.

The unfamiliar sensations that had seized Paris' body and mind were compounded by the unreality of the scenes unfolding before him in the stage-set forest, filled with strange dancing shadows cast by the orange glow of the torches.

In the clearing just beyond the fence, three satyrs had 'skinned' half a dozen of the long-haired slaves and suspended them by wrists and ankles from the lower branches of a sturdy olive tree. Their limbs were spread-eagled so that their anus' were clearly visible, like little round 'o's of astonishment. Two of the slaves had been suspended upside down, their buttocks conveniently thrust outwards at waist height.

Years of bloodlust in the arena had blended the sexual appetites of the gladiators with a taste for violence. In order to extract the maximum pleasure from their victims, they were first subjecting them to various forms of torture. Two of the horned and hairy figures had ripped switches from the tree and were meting out a thorough beating to their helpless victims. It was evident from the welts and lacerations clearly visible on the smooth and previously unblemished bodies of the slaves, as well as from their cries of pain, that this was no game. The gladiators were delivering the strokes with the brutal force of trained fighters. At the same time, the pleasure they were deriving from the exercise was evident from their leering expressions and the sturdy erections which curved up from their hairy thighs, foreskins drawn back to reveal cockheads glistening wetly in the torch-light.

The third gladiator had already penetrated his victim, one of the unfortunates who had been suspended upside down. As he roughly shafted the slave's exposed hole, he drew shrieks of agony from the lad by pulling roughly on his balls, plucking out tufts of his pubic hair and twisting the white shaft of his prick until it glowed an angry shade of crimson.

While he was observing these activities, Paris felt a scrambling of hairy thighs against his ass cheeks as Niceros adjusted his footing in order to get a better purchase up his back-passage. In this new position, the gladiator managed to force his cock a few crucial inches further into Paris' guts, lifting the boy's ass clean off the stile, so that it hung in the air, skewered on the man's rigid pole.

Though Paris' rectum was still clamped tight around Niceros' thick shaft, it had loosened and lubricated sufficiently to allow the gladiator to pull out to the rim of his glans with each stroke, plunging back into the boy with full force up to the hilt.

The glow in Paris' vitals intensified, expanding in waves to his arms and legs, until it became a tingling in his toes and fingertips. But then it seemed to spread further, reaching out into the forest so that, as he watched the gladiators' pricks pounding the fuckholes of the slaves lashed helplessly to the olive tree, he felt as though he were caught up intimately in their sensations: he could feel both the vicious thrusting of the gladiators and the aching assholes of the slaves.

Now the glow seemed to encompass the entire forest scene, making him a part of frantic couplings and penetrations that he could not see but could sense were taking behind rocks, in the shadows of trees, under bushes and in the mouths of caves.

In an instant, Paris felt the atmosphere in the fantasy forest alter imperceptibly but completely. It was as though a sudden gust of wind had blown through it, although not a leaf had stirred. Was it the passage of a god? Of Priapus himself, perhaps? Now the cries of the chase had been silenced to be replaced by a mood of rapt concentration. Only low grunts and growls sounded in the glades as the hunters sacrificed the hunted to the god, devouring and enjoying their prey. The moans of the victims could also be heard, as, abandoning all resistance, they surrendered themselves to be consumed.

As though the torches had all flared up at once, Paris became aware of vistas of pricks gleaming in the firelight, flashing between white buttocks and red lips, not just in the clearing before him but beyond, stretching into infinity. A domino-chain of pleasure had been set in motion, one climax triggering another in a vast communal orgasm.

The growing urge Paris had been feeling to bear down on Niceros' thrusting pole suddenly became intolerable. The boy surrendered all control of his bowels as his rectal muscles went into spasm and he experienced a kind of anal orgasm. Paris could felt his fuckhole take on a will of its own as it alternately clutched and released Niceros' thrusting organ, which responded by hammering away at the boy's guts like a battering ram. The increased friction lit a fire in Paris' prostate and sent a bolt of pleasure the length of the his cock, now stiff as a lightening rod, where it catapulted from his cock-slit in foaming streams of semen.

The entire forest seemed to fold up into blackness and Paris felt himself hurtling backwards and downwards. At the same time he was aware of a deep staccato growling just behind his head which rapidly grew louder and became a series of fierce roars. As Paris' fuckhole clutched convulsively around the gladiator's massive rod, it provided the final stimulus required to breach the dam of the gladiator's lust, releasing a salty deluge into the boy's gizzards.

For some time all was stillness and silence. Paris heard cries and moans all around him, but dimly as though in a dream. The only thing that seemed real was the weapon which was still poised rigid in his belly. He could already feel it stirring again and begin to slide slowly in and out of his hole, its course smoothed by the sticky libation it had already emptied into Paris' guts. Images of all-powerful Jupiter ravishing the shepherd boy Ganymede filled the youth's dreams as he slipped into unconsciousness.

CHAPTER 4

Paris awoke, as he had done every morning for the past few weeks, in Lucius' bed chamber. His first thought was to wonder how he got there. His recollections of the previous night's debaucheries tapered off into a blank. But the insistent ache in his bowels evoked his rape at the hands of Niceros the gladiator in vivid detail. It disturbed him to feel a stab of excitement at the memory. If possible, Lucius must never know anything about what had happened.

Had his lover taken part in the forest hunt? Paris wondered. He doubted it. As soon as Lucius had realised what his father had planned - and that Paris was to be delivered into other men's hands - the boy was sure that his possessive lover would not have wished to witness the event.

As he lay there musing, it struck Paris that there was something odd about the situation. How could life have returned to normal so quickly after the bizarre events of the banquet? Even stranger, however, was the fact that, though he was in Lucius' bed, his lover was absent: Paris had become accustomed to waking in the other man's tight embrace.

He did not have to wonder long. The door of the chamber flew open. Lucius stood there for a moment, staring. Beyond him Paris glimpsed Pollux peering over the young man's shoulder, a surprisingly concerned look on his normally bovine features.

As Lucius stepped towards him and the light caught his face, Paris saw that the dark cheeks were streaked with tears. He sprang from the bed in alarm. 'Father has sold you to Corax,' Lucius blurted out, choking on the words. 'You are to leave today for the gladiator school in Pompeii.'

Events moved rapidly - too fast for Lucius and Paris to spend another moment alone. A second after Lucius entered, two of Diogenes' bodyguards burst into the room behind him, just giving Paris time to fasten his sandals before marching him down to the main courtyard at the front of the villa. Four armed guards from the school were already waiting.

Roughly, they bundled the slave on to a cart, chaining him by both ankles and wrists, so that he was practically immobile. Paris grimly recalled his first visit to the school and the slave who had broken his own neck.

Pollux followed mutely after his former charge, trotting behind the cart until it turned out of the gate and into the dusty country lane. Although he had faithfully performed his duty to his master, never letting Paris out of his sight in the weeks since he had arrived at the villa, the ex-gladiator had clearly developed an affection for the boy.

As the cart trundled off down the road, Lucius suddenly tore out of the gate, distraught. Paris guessed that he had been making a last attempt to change his father's mind. The boy realised, however, that the decision had been taken a long time ago. He recalled how Diogenes and Corax had been discussing him that day at the gladiator school and he was sure now that the deal had been hatched on that occasion.

Watching Lucius sink to the ground by the gate, Paris realised that his lover's tears were not just tears of sorrow but also of anger and bitterness. For weeks now, he had been bragging how he could get anything he wanted out of his father. Paris was as good as his, he claimed. Diogenes had happily played along, knowing all the while how much sharper the blow would be when it fell. He had shown his son once and for all that he was sole emperor in his household.

The cart entered the city by the Roman gate. As it bumped noisily down the main street towards the gladiator school, Paris caught sight of Publius eating and drinking outside a tavern with a group of other soldiers. He saw the man look up, following Paris with his gaze, a goblet frozen halfway to his lips at the sight of the chains. The boy's destination was evident to any citizen of Pompeii.

The light clatter of wooden practice weapons echoed from the walls of the palaestra as Paris was led inside the gladiator school. He was manacled hand and foot, although, surrounded as he was by four burly guards, any attempt at escape would have been futile.

As he was led along the portico which stretched down one of the long sides of the courtyard, Paris recognised a number of familiar faces from the night before. Although they were now shorn of their horns and hairy flanks, the leers which lent them the authentic look of satyrs had not changed. Niceros let out a roar as he spotted the boy and, planting the handle of his sword against his crotch, jerked it up and down in a crude gesture. Paris could not stop his blushes, to his own shame and fury. A number of the gladiators spotted the lad's reaction and laughed coarsely, exchanging knowing looks.

'What are they sending us now?' demanded one hairy brute of his sparring partner as Paris passed by. 'Kids? A pretty boy like that won't last five seconds in the arena. It'll be women next!'

'So who's complaining?' agreed his fellow gladiator, a retiaraius who fought with a net and trident. 'Boys and women may not be much use in the arena, but I can think of plenty of things do with them after hours. Like to sit on this, boy?' he yelled at Paris, with a vulgar thrust of his crotch, where the man's thick tool was clearly outlined against the thin material of his loincloth.

To Paris' relief, the party reached the door of his cell. The guards shoved him into the narrow dark room and the heavy door slammed behind him, cutting off the jeers of the men.

Now, however, in the chilly darkness, the hopelessness of his situation struck him like a blow to the stomach. He had always believed he could face any challenge. But the mockery of the gladiators had undermined his confidence.

To be sold to the gladiator school was tantamount to a death sentence. And the gladiators were right: he was just a boy, not even fully grown. The typical gladiator, however – this was certainly true of champions - was a hulking brute, more animal than human, hardened in body and mind.

Paris paced the small cell. If only Lucius had listened to him and fetched his documents when he had asked him to, he would have proved long ago that he was a freedman and he would not be here. Even if he managed to retrieve the scrolls now - and he knew he must try - Corax would do everything in his power to hold on to him given that he had probably paid Diogenes a tidy sum. What was it the crafty old villain had said to Paris? 'You would earn the price of a small farm at the slave market.'

Lucius' cockiness and unwillingness to listen - even to someone who really loved him - had led to disaster. But Paris' feelings softened as he remembered his last glimpse of the young man weeping by the gate. Surely he had learned his lesson. Even now, if they could only get hold of Paris' documents and take them to the authorities, it was still possible for his freedom to be restored. He must try to get a message to his lover. Perhaps Lucius was on his way to see him even now, he thought with a sudden burst of hope.

Paris sat down on the hard narrow bed, the only piece of furniture in the room, which was without windows or adornment. In the meantime, he had to survive in this place, a prison in which all the inmates were condemned men, the date of execution known only to the gods. He must train hard, he thought, toughen his body and mind. He could run and move fast - skills that he knew, from many hours watching the games, were invaluable in the arena.

The boy turned expectantly as he heard a key creaking in the rusty lock. Could this be Lucius already? He blinked at the dark figure standing against the midday sunlight. No, this man was too broad and besides, his head was completely shaved. With a sinking of his heart, Paris realised that his visitor was the lanista, Corax.

Determined to make a good impression on the trainer, Paris leapt to his feet, drawing himself to his full height.

'Welcome to my school,' Corax barked. 'Do as you are told and you will live. There is no place for rebels here. In our oath, we vow to endure the most terrible of deaths rather than disobey. I survived more than a hundred fights myself, I know that those who listen and blindly obey survive. If you do, you will find me a fair master. I reward service and punish rebellion.'

'I want to listen and learn,' said Paris quickly.

'Ah, so eager,' observed Corax, arching a black eyebrow. 'Diogenes said you were willing...given the right situation.'

'I know I have much to learn,' added Paris.

'You think so?' said Corax gruffly. 'The reports I have heard - and not just from your former master - suggest that you already know a great deal.'

'I want to train as a gladiator,' Paris continued enthusiastically. 'I need to spend many hours in the palaestra. But I know that, with the help of the gods, I can build up my strength and learn the necessary skills to become a worthy member of your school.'

'A useful member, certainly,' Corax interjected.

'So when do I start?' asked Paris.

'Soon, very soon,' said the lanista, 'but for the moment, I suggest you get some rest. You will need all your strength for the programme we have planned for you.'

'So what am I to be,' demanded the boy - 'a retiarius? I think I could handle a net well - and I can run fast. Although I always favoured the myrmillones. They wear such fine armour,' he smiled. 'And I am skilled at handling a sword.'

'I believe so,' Corax said with a short laugh. 'A myrmillo, then. Let it be a myrmillo.'

For the rest of the day, Paris was left alone in his cell. The only light filtered through the bars of the small window in his cell door.

He dozed most of the day to the unflagging sound of the wooden weapons, chattering away like crickets. Each time he woke, the patch of sky he glimpsed through the bars had changed colour, from azure, to rose to deep purple, to ultramarine.

In the evening, he was brought a meal which was surprisingly hearty. At least the food is good in this prison, he thought wryly, as he tucked into a thick barley broth filled with chunks of tender lamb.

The palaestra was silent now. In the distance, he could hear the sound of raucous laughter - probably the gladiators enjoying their evening meal. Torch-light filtered through the bars, blocked out from time to time by the shadow of a passing sentry. Paris dozed off again until he was woken by furtive sounds, quite different from the sentry's regular tread.

There were whispers, tinkling sounds, and for an instant he smelt a woman's heavy perfume. Paris smiled. He had heard tales of the nocturnal visits gladiators received from rich matrons - and indeed from wealthy men - eager to sample their legendary prowess. The boy could still feel the nagging ache in his rectum which testified to the truth of that reputation. He wondered if Lucius might take advantage of these nocturnal comings and goings to pay him a visit and lay there for a while expectantly, unable to fall asleep.

The fatigue of the previous night's carousing must have finally got the better of him, because the next thing he knew, his cell was filled with light from torches and with guards. He was lifted bodily from the bed, his feet hardly touching the ground as he was hustled along the portico to a brightly torch-lit area in one corner of he palaestra. A number of frames and machines designed for the purpose of exercise and fighting practice were laid out on the sandy surface.

Among them stood several gladiators, dressed only in brief loincloths, their hugely muscled upper bodies gleaming with oil and sweat. They stood still and expectant, their eyes fixed on Paris as he sped towards them.

As the guards abruptly released him, the boy's feet hit the ground sharply and he tottered for a second. He found himself face to face with Corax.

'So, boy, you said you wanted to listen and learn,' the lanista rasped with a thin smile. 'Now is your chance to show that you meant it. You have been brought here in order to provide an important service to the members of the school. Many of my men enjoy the love of boys. My philosophy, the philosophy of this school, is that as long as my men are happy, they will give me of their best in the arena. So, you see, you have a very important task to perform here. Make sure you do it well.'

Corax moved away, then turned back sharply. 'Remember what I told you today: only those who obey blindly, survive.' He held Paris' gaze for a few seconds before striding off into the darkness.

Paris was faced with a terrible dilemma. If he performed this so-called service to the men, perhaps he would be able to persuade the lanista to let him train for the arena. If he refused, he would certainly not be granted another chance. The boy knew he could give the gladiators what they wanted. Now he had to swallow his pride and accept this final humiliation. He was less than a slave; he was a common prostitute. Compared to this, to be a gladiator was an honourable profession.

No sooner had these thoughts flashed through his mind, than two of the gladiators laid hold of him and dragged him towards a wooden vaulting horse. They pulled his torso along the padded leather top and tied his arms to the forelegs of the horse so that his head jutted forward. Meanwhile strong hands were already lashing his ankles to the back legs of the horse, while another gladiator was sawing roughly at Paris' clothing with a dagger.

Although they performed these tasks in silence, Paris could sense the lustful anticipation of the men in their laboured breathing. How many of them were there, he wondered - he had not thought to count them. Certainly there must have been around a dozen men standing in the palaestra when he arrived there. Was he expected to satisfy them all?

A callused palm fell on one of Paris' butt-cheeks with a loud crack, causing the boy to jump with surprise. There was a burst of raucous laughter behind him.

'So you like your boys rosy-cheeked do you Mamertinus?' called out one of the men.

A stinging blow fell on the other cheek. 'Yes, I like an ass to be good and hot before I fuck it,' grunted Mamertinus. 'Red hot. Anyone going to help me?'

He had barely finished his invitation when a dozen massive hands left their imprints on Paris upturned buttocks, raining blow after blow till the twin globes glowed scarlet. Even the exposed crack burned a savage red under the silky fringe of blond hair which surrounded the bud of Paris' hole.

'Red as the rising sun - just the way I like it,' a rough voice bellowed in a thick Thracian accent. 'Make way boys - I'm going to fuck the sun.'

'And I'm going to screw the moon as it descends behind Vesuvius,' Mamertinus responded. 'So get a move on, Thrax, or it'll have set before I get round to it.'

'Wait a minute,' boomed a voice Paris recognised only too well. 'That ass is mine - I go first.' Instinctively, Paris felt his sphincter twitch at the sound of Niceros' voice.

'You'll get your turn, Niceros,' bellowed Thrax pushing his colleague aside with a huge hairy forearm. 'We all know you've had him. You've talked enough about it. Perhaps you should have kept quiet. Now you've whetted our appetites and we all want to try him for ourselves.'

For a moment, it looked as though a fight could break out, but, though they were wild beasts, these men, like lions in the circus, knew that they were under the watchful eye of their trainer. With a snarl, Niceros made way for the other gladiator.

Paris felt hard flesh, like a blunt arrowhead, press against his anus. 'Right boy. Relax and this won't hurt a bit.' Paris felt the arrowhead begin to press its way slowly into his flesh. 'Would I lie, boys?' demanded Thrax, drawing a chorus of rough laughter from his companions.

'No, Thrax,' they shouted.

'You'll forget you ever had a wrinkle in your ass, I'll stretch you so tight, boy,' strained Thrax.

The gladiator had been pushing for some seconds, yet Paris could still feel his ring of muscle expanding to admit the head. He braced himself for the pain that was to come. The lips of his hole were still tender after the previous night's pounding and, as the slippery tip of Thrax's cockhead passed over the threshold of his rectum, Paris could feel every fold in the man's foreskin as it peeled slowly back. The glans thus exposed was so slippery with natural lubrication that, to Paris' astonishment, the entire head popped into his anal cavity as easily as an oyster slides down a glutton's throat.

The rigid pillar that followed might not have been constructed to the monstrous proportions of Niceros' murderous weapon, but it was rock-hard and of generous girth, and its slow, steady progress gave Paris the impression that it reached as far as his stomach. Thrax rocked his powerful hips so that his pole plunged full-length in and out of Paris' ass.

Meanwhile, Mamertinus, growing impatient, skirted round the horse and plunged his rigid staff down the youth's gullet. For some minutes, Mamertinus and Thrax matched one another's strokes in speed and strength - one pulling out as the other plunged in - so that Paris felt he was transfixed on a spit like a roasting pig. Without coming, Thrax withdrew with a squelch. Immediately Paris felt another rigid member penetrate his back passage, arching inwards and upwards. Enraged by the heat of the previous man's dick and the copious mingled juices already lubricating the boy's fuckhole, the gladiator began to pump away furiously.

Seized with a new idea, Mamertinus whipped his rigid rod from Paris' mouth and whirled round, jamming his asshole against the boy's still-open mouth. The man's tiny pucker was surrounded by a stubbly ass-beard. Paris was surprised at the fragrant aroma which greeted his nostrils.

His lips already dripped with the saliva stimulated by Mamertinus' cock, and the boy slavered greedily over the tasty and spotless little knot of skin, as neat as a belly-button. He drew long slow strokes over the whole anal area with the flat of his tongue, then flicked rapid vertical lines across the pucker with the tip. Slowly he began to tease the tiny creases, urging them to unfold, brushing his own lips softly against the pursed lips of the man's ass. It took some minutes of lapping at the tight hole, however, before it blossomed into a moist and tender flower. Paris gently ran his tongue over the undulating petals of ripe flesh as the gladiator's opening shyly unfolded.

Just as he did this, Mamertinus' rear-end was roughly levered aside and Paris found himself staring at another man's crack. The lips of this hole were meaty and generous, gathered into a myriad of thick pleats, and surrounded by a shaggy bush of abundant matted curls. The odour from this man was musky, acrid even, though Paris did not have a chance to hesitate as, bending double, the gladiator thrust his already winking sphincter against the boy's tongue.

By this point a third cock and then a fourth had imprinted their varying widths and lengths on Paris' asshole. By now it had become so elastic and well-lubricated that even Niceros' gargantuan tool would have slipped in up to the hilt without being distinguishable from the others. Indeed Paris was pretty certain it already had. His own throbbing erection ground against the soft leather of the horse as cock after cock rammed into him.

Paris was further intoxicated by a heady mixture of powerful aromas: hairy assholes; the hot sweat he could feel dropping onto his back from the heaving chests of the men fucking him; pre-cum glistening on the forests of phalluses that swayed around him; and the strong, mysterious scent of male sex that hung heavily in the air, emanating from these lumbering bodies. Half-men, half-beasts, thought Paris – recalling their costumes of the previous night.

It was with bestial intensity, that they shoved their engorged members down his throat and up his rear end, roughly jostling one another for access to the boy's mouth and ass. Maddened with frustration and communal lust, the gladiators' laughter and jests had faded now to be replaced by furious panting, rough growls and rasping exhalations. When Paris was able to glimpse a face, he saw it furrowed with furious concentration. For these men, only the moment existed - tomorrow they could be dead. And for each of them, the only thing that mattered in this moment was to implant their seed in Paris' tender mouth or hole.

One after another with soft roars or sobbing groans, they plunged into him with desperate urgency, emptying their ball-sacs deep within his throat and guts. Their passions enraged by the sights, sounds and smells of one another's lust, they immediately crowded round both ends of the boy to inseminate him for a second or third time. Now their eyes had the glassy look of preying birds or animals feeding on their victims. It was not blood that flew, but the mixed semen of many men as they tore again and again into Paris' body.

For Paris, the nights became days and days nights. In the small hours, the guards would fling him exhausted, semi-conscious, on his bed. Most days the chorus of wooden weapons chirped away ceaselessly. Two or three times a week, the gladiators would be taken to the large palaestra near the amphitheatre and silence would reign in the school. But, noisy or quiet, Paris lay slumped on his bed, oblivious to everything. In the evening, the slaves who brought him his meal would have to shake him awake. Later, they would bring him a jug and a bowl of water so that he could prepare himself for the rigours to come.

After some weeks of this routine, Paris became dimly aware that he was slipping into a dreamlike state. He had always been used to regular exercise in the palaestra. Without it, he was weak and listless. He feared that his body would soon become soft and feminine. While this would no doubt please the gladiators who nightly used him for their pleasure, it would surely spoil his chances of ever becoming one of them.

One evening, he enquired of the slave who brought him his meal why he was not allowed out of his cell - at least to take some exercise. 'If you were permitted to wander among the men, it might cause fights. Corax uses you, and other slaves like you, as a reward for good service. If the gladiators were to see you around every day, they would lose interest.'

With a determined effort, Paris managed to jerk himself out of his stupor. Before bathing each evening, he began to spend some time in vigorous exercise, thickening his arms and legs, broadening his shoulders and deepening his chest.

Sometimes at night, while he waited to be summoned to perform his duties, Paris' heart would quicken as he heard the sound of unfamiliar footsteps in the portico outside his cell. Could it be Lucius, finally coming to visit him? Usually he felt a pang of disappointment as the footsteps passed on.

Occasionally, however, he would hear the key turn in the lock only to see one of the gladiators shuffling shyly through the doorway, under the watchful eye of a guard. They would smile awkwardly and present him with a small gift of food, jewellery - even of money. It amused him to see how infatuated these rough men had become with him. Though his encounters with these warriors seemed to him coarse and unfeeling, apparently he brought a note of tenderness into the unrelenting harshness of their existence.

Nearly two months had passed since his arrival at the school, but still Lucius did not come. Could it be that his lover was even more weak-willed than Paris had imagined and had conceded defeat in the face of his father's wiles?

Without his help, Paris would never be able to prove that he was a freed man. It seemed that the only way open to him was to serve the lanista so well that he might eventually be allowed to train for the arena. Paris knew that, at least to some extent he had passed his initial test when Corax visited him one evening in his cell.

'I have had good reports from the men,' said Corax. 'You satisfy them. That is why I bought you and so I, too, am pleased.'

Paris realised that his assessment of the man had been right: Corax was basically a merchant – trading in the lives of men. His main concern was value for money. Paris had proved his worth in one area. Now he had to convince the lanista that he could also be of value in another.

'It seems, from all I hear, that you enjoy your work.'

'I don't consider what I do here to be work.'

'Ah,' smiled Corax. 'You enjoy it that much.'

'No, I don't enjoy it at all,' added Paris hastily. 'This is certainly not what I would choose to do. I am no prostitute' - he pronounced the word with distaste – 'but I hoped that if I could prove to you that I was prepared to obey, you may let me train for the arena. I promise I would not disappoint you there either.'

Corax laughed. 'So you think because you know how to surrender you will be able to attack? Well, we shall see. You will not be a boy forever and sooner or later the men will tire of you.' Corax ran his hand over Paris' shoulder and nodded approvingly. You seem to be filling out with the good food we are giving you: maybe you could be trained as a fighter. Who knows. Next week, the Apollo games begin. Our gladiators will be taking part and I have decided that you shall come with us. You will add beauty to the opening procession in the arena - and you will begin to learn - if you want to, that is.'

Paris' eyes were shining. 'I do,' he answered, his voice firm and strong.

The heavy doors flew open and Paris, at the head of the procession of gladiators, stepped blinking from darkness into the glare of the arena. The clear morning sunlight bounced off the white marble of the stands and the still-unblemished sand which stretched away at Paris' feet.

The crowd leaped to its feet with an exultant cry. The July games were dedicated to Apollo, and Corax had had the bright idea of dressing Paris as the golden god. This had been a popular choice with the gladiators. For many of them, the young man already represented the qualities typical of the deity - warmth, love, youth, even healing. He was sure to bring down the blessings of Apollo upon them for the duration of the games held in his honour.

With his long blond tresses crowned with a circlet of golden rays, Paris was the embodiment of the youthful god, instantly recognisable to the crowd. He wore the briefest of tunics in a semi-transparent cloth of spun gold. The outlines of his body, which had begun to bulge with hard muscle in recent months, were clearly visible. The triangular shadow of his carefully trimmed blond pubic bush could be glimpsed through the flimsy material. The heavy swing of his cock, which had matured and thickened since Paris had arrived at the school, was also evident. A trio of pretty slaves held a long train of a heavier gold material behind him, while a fourth held a golden parasol over his head.

The populace yelled its approval, throwing flowers and tickets of numbered bone. Paris moved around the elliptical arena, to the blare of trumpets and the squeaks of a slightly out-of-tune water organ, followed by the gladiators of the school. Most of them were great favourites of the people who cried out their names with shouts of encouragement: 'Let him have it, Niceros!' 'Give it to him, Thrax!'

Considering that most of the mob had bet far more than they actually possessed, it was hardly surprising that their excitement and expectation had reached fever-pitch. That morning, as he had been carried by cart through the long straight street which led to the amphitheatre, Paris had seen the city again for the first time since his arrival at the school almost two months earlier.

The days of the games were declared public holiday and the streets were packed with citizens and visitors from the surrounding towns. Summer was always a busy season in this popular seaside region – and the games were an additional attraction. Paris could see frantic exchanges of money and IOU's in each tavern and on every street-corner, as the devotees of the games backed their favourites with muttered prayers to the goddess Fortuna. More than a hundred pairs of gladiators were to meet in combat over the next few days.

As Paris approached the open gates which led back into the dark cells under the stands, he glanced up for a moment towards the crowd. His heart leapt as his eyes met those of Lucius, staring down at him with a mixture of fear and longing. There was no time for a signal to pass between the two men, and, anyway, Paris knew that, for the moment, he was Apollo and had to behave with fitting solemnity. He stepped back through the gates and into the shadows.

The games were sponsored by Nigidius Maius, one of Pompeii's richest citizens. He was famed as 'the prince of impresarios' and a spectacular programme had been promised. The first morning consisted of bull-fights and, as Paris waited with the other gladiators in the dark labyrinth of cages, chambers and theatrical machinery under the stands, he could hear the thundering of hoofs and the light patter of agile human footsteps outside. The constant roar of the crowd would rise whenever the bullfighter attacked, lowering to a long note of trepidation or a sharp cry of fear when he was charged by the crazed beast.

Ben Elliott

When the whole crowd burst into a deafening roar, it meant that blood had been spilt. Whether it was the bull's or the fighter's was not immediately clear. On several occasions, however, blood-spattered men would be rushed along the narrow corridors on stretchers. Chambers had been specially set aside where surgeons from the school's infirmary would probe the wounds with their long sharp instruments of silver and bronze before stitching them up with thick black thread.

In addition to the noise of the games, the backstage area was constantly filled with the sounds of frightened animals, scheduled to take part in hunting scenes. These mingled with the screams of condemned prisoners due to be slaughtered in the lunch break, before the gladiatorial contests that were the major draw.

As the hour for the combats approached, the corridors backstage buzzed with activity. The warriors and their assistants polished their weapons and armour till they shone like mirrors. Officials checked the weapons for their sharpness. A slave touched up Paris' own costume, placing the circlet on his head and adjusting the golden train.

With a rustle of black silk, a ghoulish figure brushed past Paris: it was Charon, the boatman of the underworld - or, rather a man dressed to resemble him, his face painted into a twisted mask of purple and blue. His task was to confirm the death of a gladiator by striking him on the forehead with a mallet and then to supervise his removal from the arena through the Porta Libitinensis, dedicated to the goddess of death.

Turning away with a shudder, Paris found himself looking into the laughing eyes and the open smile of the soldier Publius. He was carrying his helmet under his arm, as the corridors were too low for him to wear it. As it was, he was forced to stoop slightly to avoid grazing his head on the ceiling.

'I'd like to kiss you, fair Apollo,' grinned Publius - 'if a mortal dare kiss a god, that is.'

Paris blushed fiercely. He could not help liking this soldier with the bantering words and gentle manner. 'Better not,' he whispered: 'there are guards from the school everywhere and Corax doesn't allow anyone to lay a finger on me without his permission.'

'Can I visit you at the school sometime?'

'At present, I'm not allowed visitors.'

'You must be the only who isn't. From what I hear, between sundown and sunup the gladiator school is busier than the forum on market day.'

Paris smiled. 'It does get pretty active.'

'Well,' said Publius, 'I don't see why I shouldn't try my luck. After all, this still has some influence,' he added, indicating his helmet. 'And this,' patting a leather money pouch hanging at his belt.

'I would be glad to see you,' said Paris, his eyes meeting those of the soldier. Everyone else appeared to have abandoned him - he needed a friend. And this man seemed trustworthy and steadfast.

Paris had an important part to play in the afternoon's events. He was seated on a throne at the edge of the arena throughout the gladiatorial contests so that he could be seen by both the crowd and the combatants. When each pair entered, they would bow both to Nigidius, as editor of the games, and to Paris, who responded with what he hoped was a suitably divine nod.

Thrax, who had become one of his most devoted admirers, stood proudly by his side when he was not fighting and explained the proceedings.

'The crowds are such fools,' he growled in Paris' ear. 'They think that these bouts are fairly fought when in fact the results have often been decided long ago by the editor and the lanista, who will both make a fortune from the day's betting.'

'You mean that some of the gladiators deliberately lose?'

'Of course, all this huffing and puffing is just for show. As long as the people get a little blood, a flesh wound, they are happy. Look at all my scars. Perhaps two at most were serious wounds. The others were for show. Of course we can put on a good fight when we need to, but most of the time we're actors and this is a theatre. One of us is famous because he growls and leaps like a tiger, another because he trumpets and charges like an elephant. Some of us play the hero, others the villain. That's what the crowd wants and that's what we give 'em.'

When it was Thrax's turn to fight, he roared and stormed with the best of them. He was the victor of his bout and, as he swaggered back across the arena towards Paris, he brandished his left arm, slashed from shoulder to elbow, while the spectators roared their approval. As Thrax reached Paris, he bent in a solemn bow before the boy-god. Then, peeking up at him, gave a sly wink.

Having received his prize-money from the editor, Thrax returned to Paris' side, proudly showing off the bag of coins. 'Five of those and you could buy your freedom,' he nodded sagely.

'How many wins have you had?' enquired Paris.

'Oh twenty, thirty. I lost count.'

'Why are you still here, then?' asked Paris in surprise.

'It's a good life,' mused Thrax. 'Glory, money, fine armour. A constant supply of boys and women.'

After months cooped up in his cell, Paris felt quite dizzy by the end of the day. Given that Paris' appearance as Apollo had been such a success, Corax decided that the boy should ride back with him in his litter, rather than travel back by cart with the gladiators. Wild with excitement after the afternoon's displays, the rabble pressed around them, cheering and reaching out to touch Paris for good luck. The litter made slow progress.

Suddenly, one face stood out clearly from the hundreds turned towards him. It was Lucius and Paris was overjoyed to see that his lover was struggling through the press of bodies, trying to reach the litter. He even seemed to be calling out, though his words were lost in the uproar.

As Lucius drew within arm's length of the litter, two of the school guards stepped forward and roughly pushed him back. Paris turned to watch the young man frantically struggling to free himself.

'Wave to your worshippers,' growled Corax, scanning the crowd with a cold glare. 'For today, at least, you are not a man but a god.'

That night as he lay in his cell recalling the day's events, Paris' thoughts kept returning to Lucius' despairing expression as he watched his lover being carried off in the litter.

The corridor outside his cell was much busier than usual: the excitement of the games had obviously inflamed the passions of the wealthy men and women of Pompeii and made the attractions of the gladiators even more irresistible than usual. The tripping of feet and the tinkling of jewellery seemed to pass by in a continuous procession. At least half a dozen different perfumes filtered into Paris' cell as the wearers hurried anxiously to the rough embraces of their champions.

Paris sat up as he detected a change in this familiar pattern of sounds. The clink of trinkets had stopped right outside his door. A key was creaking in the rusty lock and a gust of cinnamon blew into the room on the warm night air. A tall figure completely veiled in a shimmering gown of midnight blue stepped into the cell.

The door closed silently and the key was firmly turned in the lock.

'Madam,' cried Paris, leaping to his feet. 'I fear you have been misinformed.'

The figure raised her head. Paris recognised the dark eyes flashing beneath the heavy veil.

'I think not,' came a voice that was startlingly deep.

The veil was thrown back and Paris' heart turned over for joy as he realised that the mysterious visitor was none other than Lucius.

CHAPTER 5

Paris' first impulse was to throw himself into his lover's arms, but Lucius held him back.

'Help me remove these,' he pleaded in a whisper. 'I will need them to get out undetected.'

Paris could not suppress a giggle as he carefully drew the blue robe over Lucius' head, only to find another elaborate gown, the kind a lady might wear for a dinner party, underneath. Last of all, came silken under-garments.

'The disguise had to be complete,' explained Lucius, lifting off an elaborate wig of twisted plaits. He slipped bangles of silver and jade from his wrists. 'Sometimes, visitors are searched. Could you unclasp my neck-lace?'

Having unhooked the heavy gold torque, Paris placed his arms around the other man's neck. He was touched that Lucius had taken so much trouble to reach him. 'Surely you didn't manage this all by yourself?'

'Bion helped me,' Lucius admitted. 'You know, he really cares about you. He wept for days after you were brought here. I did, too, but I have to confess that my tears were partly of wounded pride. I realised how eas-ily I had been duped. I was so sure I could twist my father round my little finger. But I underestimated him. I've always despised him. I could never understand how he had risen from slavery to such wealth. I was beginning to believe that his devotion to the gods had truly brought him good fortune. Now I realise it was sheer cunning.'

'Does he knew you are here?'

'Of course not. In fact he has forbidden me to ever see you again. And I think I have convinced him that everything is finished between us. He and Corax are thick as thieves, as you know, and the guards here are under strict orders to turn me away.'

'So you took a risk by coming to see me in this way,' said Paris, taking Lucius face between his hands. The last of the woman's undergarments had been folded neatly on the bed and now Lucius stood before Paris, exposed in his full masculine beauty. Slipping his tunic from his shoulders, Paris fell to his knees before his lover. His heart beating hard, he took Lucius' silken cock reverently in his hands. It throbbed into life at his touch, releasing a deep sigh from Lucius' lips.

Paris felt cool slender fingers run gently through his hair, caressing his scalp. Paris stroked the dark, crinkled ball-sac and watched the fully erect cock jump and quiver in response. Now it was his turn to sigh as he moved his lips towards Lucius' manhood, inhaling deeply the unique rich aroma of his lover's sex-organ. He began to kiss the vertical pillar from the taut foreskin to the musky seed-bags. He could feel the heat of the member against his cheek and ran his fingers through the tangle of wiry dark hair that clustered so thickly around the base of his lover's proud column.

A shudder ran through Lucius' body as Paris took the man-rod firmly between his lips and pushed them greedily down its full length, his nose pressed into the forest of hair. The boy constricted his throat so that, with the slightest movement of his head, he could massage the entire shiny surface of Lucius' exposed glans. The man's legs began to tremble with the intensity of the pleasure, so long awaited. Paris made a circling movement with the root of his tongue, tormenting the underside of Lucius cockhead still held in the vicelike grip of his gullet. Lucius' long muscular legs shook like saplings in a storm, his hands clutching convulsively at Paris' skull.

Continuing the movement of his tongue, Paris began to rock his head rapidly backwards and forwards, adding a second, rougher stimulus to cockhead and shaft. At the same time, he took Lucius' balls firmly between the fingers of each hand, working the wormlike tangle of ducts with enough pressure to cause a dull ache that stopped just short of pain. Paris felt the balls softening under his skilful fingertips. Although he was trying to keep as quiet as possible, Lucius could not prevent low sobs and choking moans escaping from his lips. The lean, knotted muscles of his legs had gone into spasm and his knees were beginning to buckle.

'I want to have you,' he whispered to Paris. 'I must plant my seed in you.'

He pushed Paris face-up on to the tiny bed, pressing his ankles back and apart so that the wrinkled rosebud of the boy's arsehole stared up expectantly. Lucius dropped a well-aimed blob of spit on to the spot where he was about to plant the tree of his virility. Not that it was necessary: Paris already felt his sphincter melting with anticipation, a furrow ready to be fertilised, opening up to his lover's organ with a willingness that it showed for no other man.

Both men gasped as Lucius' cock slid into Paris' ass from shiny tip to hairy root in one swift movement of intense mutual pleasure. Paris dared not touch his prick, ramrod stiff, glossy and ripe as a bunch of grapes, every thick vein bulging. The burning and pressure of Lucius' mighty member in his fuckhole was so fierce that Paris' staff danced and quivered with a life of its own and the boy had to bite his lip to stop his load from bursting forth of its own accord.

Thrusting furiously, unable to hold back, Lucius fell forward on to Paris' chest pressing his open, panting lips to Paris' hungry mouth, shoving the boy's knees back against his shoulders. 'I...love...you,' Lucius gasped, stabbing Paris' ass with such force that it seemed he wished to pierce his lover's heart with his lance.

As Paris felt Lucius' scalding load gushing into his entrails with each rigid jerk of his rod, the boy could no longer hold back and his own sap began to overflow in matching spasms. It seemed that the convulsions in their loins would never end. Instead of bringing release, one orgasm triggered another, more intense - painful even - than the last. It was as though their passion for one another, which had been starved so long of its release, could not be satisfied.

For a time, they lay still, Paris' head against Lucius' chest, listening to the hollow thumping of the man's still-racing heart.

'For weeks, I waited for you to come to me,' Paris whispered at last. 'I had come to the conclusion that somehow your father had bribed you to give me up. Until I saw your face today at the games.'

'Nothing could ever make me do that,' Lucius insisted vehemently. 'As for my father, he has lost my respect forever. He told me why you were sent here. "Don't worry," he gloated: "your little friend is no danger - he isn't even going to be a gladiator." But I didn't give him the satisfaction of showing him how I felt. Inside, I was burning up with rage and jealousy at the thought of...what was happening to you.'

'Let's not talk about that,' said Paris softly. 'We are together now and somehow we'll be together again. I know it. And it's not so bad here. I think that soon Corax will allow me to start training for the arena. That could be one way to earn my freedom.'

'I have a few ideas of my own how we can get you out of here,' replied Lucius, tightening his grip around Paris' shoulders.

'There's one very simple way,' Paris insisted: 'do you remember I told you about my father's documents which I hid at the sanctuary of Cumae? Bring them here, or show them to the authorities, and Corax will be compelled to set me free.'

Lucius pulled away from Paris and stood up, suddenly remote. 'That would never work. Corax will find a way to disprove your claim. He paid my father an enormous sum of money for you. Only a similar sum or a larger one would induce him to release you.'

'But it could take me years to earn such an amount in the arena. And I don't see there's any chance of your father giving it to you. But my father's scrolls could free me now.'

'No,' snapped Lucius. Then, seeing Paris' expression of shock, he added more gently. 'Let me try my way first. I think I can raise the sum necessary to buy your freedom. I am prepared to do anything for you, Paris. Please let me try.'

Paris shrugged his assent. He was puzzled and a little shaken at the vehemence of Lucius' attitude. If he was prepared to do anything, why not perform this simple errand? Surely that possibility was at least worth exploring?

But he did not want to waste the little time they had together in an argument. Corax had told the boy that he would spend the night alone so as to be fresh for the games next day. Although Lucius would have to leave before dawn - his disguise might not stand the scrutiny of daylight - they still had most of the night to themselves.

Though he had only managed to grab a couple of hours sleep after Lucius' departure, Paris was already waiting when they unlocked his cell the next morning. On the way back from the amphitheatre the previous day, Corax had expressed his satisfaction with Paris' performance in the arena. The crowd had been delighted with him.

'I have decided that perhaps you could be an asset in the arena after all,' Corax observed. 'I can already see the posters: we will bill you as the gladiator Apollo.'

This was to be Paris' first day of training and he was impatient to start. Most of the gladiators were already practising hard for the games which would continue for another week. Corax himself was to supervise the first stages of Paris' education for the arena and was already waiting by the exercise machines.

Paris smiled to himself recalling how they had previously been the scene of his humiliation at the hands of the gladiators: now they would help him fight back against the hopeless situation in which the fates had placed him.

Corax was impressed at the boy's strength, speed and quick reactions. Much of the time that morning was spent practising sword strokes on a revolving dummy. Paris was a little irritated at having to do battle with a scarecrow, but was anxious to impress the lanista, so he tried not to show his frustration. The boy was concentrating so hard on the exercises set by the veteran trainer that he did not notice the tall, handsome figure quietly watching from the shadows of the portico.

'That will be all for this morning,' barked Corax after a couple of hours of intense drill. 'I think you may surprise many, both in the school and beyond,' he added with a dry smile, before striding off to his study. Paris was unable to reply. He was still bent double, struggling to catch his breath.

He started when a voice right beside him said, 'I think he's right.'

Publius was grinning down at him, looking splendid in his full uniform, helmet decorated with bobbing plumes of flaming scarlet. 'I've been watching from over there. I kept in the shadows as I didn't want to put you off. By the way,' he said in a lower tone, ' nobody knows I came just to see you. I told them that I'm a devotee of the games and wanted to watch the men training.'

Paris stood up, smiling: Publius' cheek amused him. 'Normally I would have been locked in my cell at this time. What made you think you'd get to see me?'

'I'd have found a way. Anyway, it was obvious after your reception at the games yesterday that there would be little point in keeping you hidden away. They are running a business here after all.' His expression suddenly became serious. 'From what I've seen, Paris, you have the makings of a champion. You may not have the brute strength of some of these animals here' - he nodded towards the gladiators who were still training hard in the palaestra - 'but you have something they lack to a man - intelligence. Besides you're strong and quick. Those are important qualities, too.'

'Thank you,' replied Paris: he could see that the soldier was sincere and he was heartened by his encouragement.

'I am a fighting man, too. Fighting of the serious kind - not just tricks. If you want my help in your training, you have only to ask.'

'I'm grateful for your offer, Publius. I intend to succeed in the ring. I will accept all offers of help.'

Paris' appearance at the games that day was - if anything - an even greater success than his debut. The citizens of Pompeii were expecting him and reacted with the enthusiasm they normally reserved for a favourite gladiator. In the evening, he returned in Corax's litter once again.

The boy was fired with enthusiasm after the day's excitement. 'When will I be ready to fight?' he demanded eagerly of his trainer as they rode back to the school.

'Next season, perhaps,' replied Corax vaguely. 'However, I don't intend to risk my investment in you. Any contest you take part in will be - shall we say - carefully planned.'

'Fixed you mean,' Paris shot back, reddening with shame.

Corax turned to the boy, his dark eyes filled with cold fury. 'That is a word we never use. The people expect to be entertained – and that's we do. At the price one has to pay for potential gladiators these days, I would go bankrupt if I allowed them to be slaughtered at the whim of an editor or of the people.'

'Will I ever be allowed to win?' asked Paris sullenly.

'First you must train. Then we will judge your potential.'

In order to allow him time for training, his other duties would be curtailed, Corax informed the boy. In future, he would only meet with one gladiator at a time, in his own cell and only three nights a week. The visits would be limited to two hours each. Corax himself would permit the visits to those gladiators he wished to reward. And Paris would not be forced to service anyone he particularly disliked. 'Good,' thought Paris. 'No more Niceros.'

When he heard a key scraping in the lock late that night, his first thought was that the lanista had changed his mind and that he had been sent a client. A slight figure in a cloak stepped into the cell - this was no gladiator. A ray of moonlight struck the visitor's face through the barred window in the door. To Paris' astonishment and delight he recognised his friend Bion. He leaped from the bed and embraced the slave boy, planting a hearty kiss on either cheek.

'What a delightful room,' said Bion pulling a face. He undid a jewelled fibula at his throat and tossed his cloak on to the bed. 'But, if you don't mind a suggestion, a fresco would look lovely on this wall – a seaside villa perhaps. A curtain – cloth-of-gold or something like that – might soften this wall: it's a little grim, if I may say so. And over here a porphyry statue – perhaps a satyr or a Priapus. Then, of course silk sheets and an embroidered eiderdown on the bed would be a lot more comfortable.' He accompanied these remarks with extravagant gestures, then suddenly dropped his arms to his sides, swinging round to face Paris. 'I can't bear to think of you in this place,' he said. Paris thought he noticed a glint of tears in the slave boy's eyes. 'Diogenes has always been good to me and I cannot ever imagine myself leaving his household. But what he has done to you has made me hate him.'

'What are you doing here?' asked Paris, impatiently.

'Well,' Bion confided. 'Lucius did nothing all day but complain that he couldn't wait to see you again. He wasn't able to discuss it with anyone else so he droned on and on to me. I had to finish a new tunic I've made for Diogenes to wear at the games – there are hundreds of jewels to be sewn on. Lucius nearly drove me crazy: I thought I'd never finish. One minute he was convinced that the two of you were more in love than ever. The next he was worrying that he had made a bad impression and that maybe you didn't care so much for him anymore. He wanted to visit you again tonight, but he knew that would be arouse suspicions.

'Eventually I got so tired of it all, I thought of a way to shut him up. "It's true that it would be risky for you to return the school so soon," I told him, "but there would be no harm in my bringing Paris a letter from my mistress." So here I am.'

'What's the message?' grinned Paris.

'She's so coy, that mistress of mine, that she didn't want to tell me. So I said, "Why don't you use the method most respectable matrons use to send secret messages to their lovers?" As he spoke, Bion turned away from Paris and slipped his tunic from his shoulders. 'It's written on my back. In milk. So I have no idea what it says. Oh, you need this' - he pulled a little leather pouch from his belt and handed it to Paris. 'Just sprinkle some on my shoulders and then blow on it.'

Intrigued, Paris opened the pouch and sprinkled some of the powder it contained on to the slim white shoulders of the slave. 'It's soot,' exclaimed Paris wrinkling up his nose at the sour smell. 'Yes, yes I know. It won't hurt. That's how it's done.'

Carefully, Paris sprinkled a little more of the black powder and gently blew away the excess.

'Mmmm. That's nice,' murmured Bion, leaning back against Paris' chest for a moment. 'So, what does it say? Or are you going to be all mysterious, too?'

'"Dearest",' read Paris, keeping his voice low for the benefit of passing guards. '"I want you to know that I love you and I will not rest until I have secured your freedom. Be patient and trust me, Lucius".'

Bion gave a soft whistle. 'How does he plan to do that?'

Paris sighed and sat on the bed. 'He has this idiotic idea that he can buy my freedom. I'm sure he means well – but where will he be able to lay his hands on that kind of money? He's completely under his father's thumb. And the annoying thing is that there is a much simpler way for me to win my freedom, only Lucius refuses to accept it. I just can't understand why.'

Bion crouched on the bed beside Paris. 'You know how stubborn he can be. He so enjoys playing the young master.'

'Listen, Bion, you are a good friend and I know I can trust you. I need you to run a simple errand for me and bring me an important package I hid months ago, before I arrived at Diogenes' villa. You would be giving me the most precious gift any man can give – freedom.'

'What, just by bringing you a package?'

'It contains documents proving that I am the son and heir of a freed-man.'

'Where is it – this package?'

'Would you be able to find an excuse to visit the Sybil at Cumae?'

Bion leaned back on his elbows and laughed. 'Diogenes sends me there all the time with questions for the oracle. The elections take place next week: I'm sure my master would love to have it from the lips of the Sybil that he is going to win.'

'Perfect. The package is hidden deep in the cave, where no thief would dare venture for fear of the Sybil's curse. Now listen carefully.'

Over the next few days, Paris waited anxiously for Bion's return. Fortunately, it was a busy time. The mornings began with training in the palaestra. He could tell from the way in which Corax followed him with his steely gaze that he was making good progress. Sometimes Publius was also present and afterwards made useful suggestions. The rest of the day was taken up with the games.

Occasionally, one of the gladiators would visit his cell at night, aflame with passion following a victory in the amphitheatre. Though Paris was still obliged to offer his services to the men, the guards would time these bouts of love-making carefully and give a sharp rap on the door after a couple of hours. Following these visits, Paris lay awake most of the night, wondering when Bion would come.

It was not until the eve of the eighth and final day of the games that the door of Paris' cell swung open to reveal not a gladiator but the dancing boy from Gades. Paris crossed the room in a flash. 'Where are the scrolls?' he demanded anxiously.'

The slave stared at Paris dumbly. For once, he had nothing to say.

'Didn't you get them?' Paris insisted, his voice rising.

'No,' replied Bion softly.

'What happened?' snapped Paris, shaking Bion by the shoulders.

'Wouldn't Diogenes let you go to Cumae?'

'That part was not difficult. I know my master: when I made the suggestion, he was only too eager for me to go.'

'So what went wrong. Couldn't you remember the instructions you stupid boy.'

'Oh yes, I knew them by heart. For days I repeated them while I was working. When I got to the sanctuary, I found the hiding place exactly as you described it. The stone that should have concealed the documents was there, marked with the sign you showed me. But it had been moved and the documents were gone.'

Paris turned pale. His knees buckled and he stumbled backwards on to the bed.

'But that's impossible. No one knew where the scrolls were hidden but you – and Lucius.' The two young men looked at each other – the same thought passing through their minds, though neither dared speak it. 'No, no – that's impossible,' Paris whispered aloud. Surely Lucius would never betray him. For a moment he saw his lover's face twisted with hatred and cruelty - like the mask of a fury in a Greek play. He must think, he must decide what to do. But his mind was blank. All he could see was the strange, monstrous distortion of Lucius' face.

'I must see him,' murmured Paris. 'You must tell him to come to me – as soon as possible, Bion. Tonight.'

Bion sat down beside his friend who was slumped against the wall like a man who had been run through with a sword. Paris stared at the cold flagstones with wide eyes. He began to shiver uncontrollably.

Putting his arm around Paris, Bion covered him with his cloak and drew the blond head on to his chest. After a while, Paris' shuddering subsided. Without thinking, he fumbled for the other lad's face in the dark, desperate for comfort. Bion's lips met his own and gently parted. Paris stretched out on the bed, pulling Bion down beside him. As Paris explored the firm dancer's body with his hands, Bion responded with a sweet willingness that reminded Paris of his uncle's slave, Epaphra. He was rougher with the boy than he meant to be, but Bion did not seem to mind.

Afterwards Paris lay awake though he felt the lad drop off to sleep almost immediately, his head on Paris' chest and his arms about his neck. The boy's breathing was almost imperceptible and his face in sleep was as innocent as a baby's. Paris could not bear to wake him until the patter of departing footsteps in the corridor signalled the approaching dawn.

'Don't think that I expect anything from you because of what we've done,' whispered Bion, as he slipped into his tunic. 'I can't hide the fact that I love you.' He glanced briefly at Paris with a wry smile, 'It would be pointless to deny it now.' The boy looked away again. 'I have been with many men; I was trained from childhood to give pleasure. And I don't pretend that I don't enjoy it. But the act on its own means very little. What I feel for you is different. And what we just did felt different.'

Paris, still lying on the bed, reached out for Bion's hand. The slave continued to face away from him. 'I am a slave. I was born to be a slave and I will die a slave. You are special. You were born free and one day you will be free again. I know that you can never see me as more than a friend. But that is enough for me. If ever you need my help again, I will always be ready.' Bion stared down at Paris, as if committing the moment to memory, before the sound of the sentry's footsteps caused him to move swiftly towards the door. As the guard passed, Bion called out to him through the bars.

'You will ask Lucius to come?' Paris whispered urgently as he heard the key turn in the lock.

'He will be here tonight,' replied Bion softly.

'But you must not say anything about the documents,' warned Paris.

Bion shook his head sadly. 'No this is something that only the two of you can resolve.' He turned to face Paris: 'Don't be too quick to judge him,' he said and disappeared into the corridor.

Paris sat on the bed watching the light gradually change from blue to green until the first warm rays of the sun were reflected into the cell. When the guards came to fetch him for the start of his training, he had not moved.

For the concluding ceremonies of the games, Corax had brought a choreographer down from Rome to stage a scene involving all the members of the school. The mime, which depicted the apotheosis of Apollo, was a triumph – and Paris, as Apollo, was the prime object of the crowd's rapturous applause. No one – not even Corax – guessed that the boy passed through the day in a trance, unable to think of anything but the lost documents and the part Lucius might have played in their disappearance.

That evening, a banquet was held for the gladiators at tables specially laid out in the palaestra for the occasion. Rose-covered pergolas had been set up, transforming the usual stark military atmosphere of the place into that of an elegant triclinium. Paris had no appetite for the extravagant delicacies on offer. Thrax who lay next to him on the couch showed gruff concern, but Paris offered the excuse that he had had too much sun.

The party broke up early. Corax had promised the gladiators women and boys as a reward for their performance in the amphitheatre. While the dinner was still underway, the gates of the school swung open to admit a noisy crowd of gaudily dressed prostitutes of both sexes. As they swarmed towards the tables, it seemed that the entire population of the city's seedier taverns had assembled at the school.

Chaos broke out as the prostitutes scrambled on to the couches, the gladiators grabbing at a women or boy that caught their fancy. Some wanted more than one of the same sex, while those with more sophisticated tastes chose to mix both genders. The guards weighed into the melee, where fights threatened over a particularly beautiful specimen. But there were more than enough to go round. Like all commodities in this city of abundance, ladies and gentlemen of the night were in plentiful supply.

The tables soon emptied as the gladiators dragged their chosen partners, screaming and struggling with feigned reluctance - off to their quarters or other dark corners of the school.

Paris managed to slip back to his cell in the confusion. He barely heard the roars and moans of pleasure which echoed round the palaestra from cell doorways and the shadows of porticos, but his ears immediately picked out a light tinkle of jewellery as it approached his door, some hours later. The key ground in the lock and the tall veiled silhouette stooped slightly to pass into the cell. The scent of cinnamon which had seemed so charming on Lucius' previous visit, now made Paris' gorge rise.

Lucius pulled the veil from his face and stepped towards the boy with an eager smile. 'I had planned to wait a little longer before putting this disguise to the test again, but when Bion brought your message nothing could hold me back.' He lifted the wig from his head and tossed it hurriedly on to the bed. 'Help me get out of these. You can't imagine how

I've been longing to see you again.'

Paris stood, silent and unmoving. He could tell from the young man's demeanour, that Bion had not revealed the true purpose of the urgent summons.

As he slipped the glittering blue robe from his shoulders, Lucius threw Paris a puzzled look. 'Aren't you going to give me a hand? I can't do this by myself.' Then he noticed the boy's stare, as cold and stoney as Medusa's. A flicker of fear passed across Lucius' face. 'Paris, what is it? Why are you looking at me like that?'

'I sent a messenger to the Sybil's cave at Cumae to fetch my father's documents,' said Paris slowly, without expression. His eyes were fixed on Lucius' face, searching for a reaction. He did not have to wait long. The other man's dark complexion flushed a deep terracotta. Paris continued. 'The hiding place had been disturbed and the documents were gone.'

Lucius sank on to the bed crumpling like a silk scarf dropped by the breeze. His characteristic cockiness and confidence had evaporated. Now his skin had paled to the ghastly grey of unbaked clay. In fact, Paris thought, he looked weak, pathetic, foolish even in his woman's robes and jewellery.

'You were the only one who knew were they were,' hissed Paris.

'Lucius,' he took a step towards the other man, certain now of his guilt - 'you betrayed me. How could you do such a thing after all your declarations of love?'

Lucius looked up. 'I was wrong - I know that now - but I never meant to betray you,' he pleaded. 'When you first told me about the documents, I was afraid that if you managed to get them back, I would lose you. So I had them brought to me at the villa and hid them safely away.'

'But I told you that I would never leave you. Why couldn't you have trusted me?'

'Up to that time people and things were like a child's toys to me. I had always been the master. I though that if you were free you would no longer be completely mine. But by the time I realised my mistake, it was too late.'

'What do you mean?' Paris demanded, a chill gripping his heart.

'What I didn't realise was that my father had my rooms searched regularly,' whispered Lucius, staring at the floor. 'I was so convinced that I had him round my little finger, I never even suspected what was really going on.' He looked up at Paris. 'My father found the documents.'

'So Diogenes sold me to Corax knowing that I was a freedman.'

'I think he believed you from the start - even before he had the proof,' murmured Lucius. 'It was obvious to everyone that you were no slave. But he had already promised you to Corax. So when he discovered the documents, he had no choice but to destroy them.'

'Destroy them?' exclaimed Paris, no longer concerned about being overheard by a passing guard.

'Yes,' replied Lucius weakly. 'Even before you were sold to Corax. That's why the only solution now is to buy your freedom. I have suggested to father that he should emancipate me, giving me my inheritance now. Many fathers do that with their elder sons these days.'

Paris gave a bitter laugh. 'You are so naive, Lucius. You have never understood your father and you have never understood me.' A note of vehemence entered his voice as he leaned his face close to the other man's. 'I will not be bought - even if you could raise the money, which I doubt. Haven't you realised yet that you cannot buy another man's love?'

'I know that now,' mumbled Lucius. He looked up at Paris, his dark eyes glossy with tears. 'Paris, I've changed. I know I can't buy you. But what alternative do we have? I've learned from my mistakes: give me another chance.'

Paris shrank back against the cold wall of the cell. 'No, Lucius. I loved you once and even now, for the sake of what we had, I wish you no harm. But my feelings for you are dead. I can never forgive you for what you have done. Leave me now. If we ever meet again, it will be as strangers.'

Paris strode to the door and hammered loudly to call the sentry.

Lucius stumbled to his feet, crushed by the force of Paris' words. He hurriedly replaced the wig, slightly askew, on his head. His long dark fingers shook like leaves as he drew the veil about him.

'I will never stop loving you, Paris,' whispered Lucius, turning to the other man as the sound of the sentry's footsteps echoed down the portico towards them. 'Maybe with time your hatred for me will fade and you will remember what we meant to each other.'

'I don't hate you,' replied Paris dully. 'Worse than that: I feel nothing for you.'

His shoulders hunched, Lucius turned away, hurrying off into the darkness.

CHAPTER 6

Now that the Apollo Games were over, Paris' training was to due to begin in earnest. The morning after Lucius' visit, Corax came to his cell at first light. He was accompanied by a slave who carried armour, a shield, a curved sword and a finely-carved silver helmet, its crest a golden fish: the costume of a myrmillo. Though he had not taken it seriously at the time, Corax had remembered Paris' request.

'So far, your practice has consisted of exercises to improve your strength and skills with the shield and the sword. Today you will use what you have learned in face to face combat.'

The slave fitted the armour on Paris, while Corax explained just how tightly to buckle the straps so as to allow maximum movement yet minimize nooks and crannies where a lethal sword tip could enter. One piece of armour protected his right arm and shoulder, while another covered his left leg from foot to thigh.

Paris was surprised at how much these two pieces weighed him down. Movements that had been second nature before, now required conscious effort. The splendid helmet which rested on his shoulders and covered his entire head and face was heaviest of all. To make matters worse, once it was locked into position by turning two keys just below the visor, Paris found that his field of vision was drastically reduced. He could see nothing out of the corners of his eyes. Even his frontal vision was limited, as the visor consisted of a series of holes which sliced what he saw into small pieces, like a mosaic.

Corax had matched Paris with one of the lighter gladiators, close to his own build. The other man was similarly armed, but, as an experienced fighter, scored constant hits against Paris. The swords were wooden, but Paris knew that if this had been a genuine fight in the arena, he would have died a hundred times over. Weighed down by the armour, he felt as though he were moving through quicksand. Several times, he lost his balance as a result of the effect the helmet had on his vision.

The sun began to beat down on the palaestra, making the helmet hot as a brazier. Paris' long hair was soaked with sweat, running in rivulets down his neck. The helmet was so airless, he found it increasingly difficult to breath, so that several times he almost fainted. Paris had begun the session tired and dispirited after the events of the previous few days. As he took fall after fall, and blow upon blow, he was overcome by a feeling of hopelessness. How could he have imagined that he would be able to succeed as a gladiator and win his freedom in the ring?

While the slave helped him remove his helmet at the end of the practice, he glanced over to Corax, trying to read his thoughts. As usual, the lanista's dark eyes were blank. He strode over to Paris and grasped him by the shoulder. 'It's not so easy, is it? But don't worry, you'll get used to the armour and then your real training as a myrmillo will begin.' How long would Corax's patience last, though? wondered Paris.

'What's wrong,' asked a voice at his elbow. Paris turned to see Publius gazing at him not with his usual expression of amusement, but with a look of concern. 'Oh, nothing,' mumbled Paris. 'It's my first time with armour.'

Publius shook his head firmly. 'It's not that: there's something else. I thought I could see it in your movements today and now, looking into your eyes, I am sure.'

Paris felt reassured in the soldier's presence. He was calm and strong. 'Publius, I am in terrible trouble,' Paris whispered urgently. 'Come and see me tonight. If you can get past the guards.'

The soldier smiled reassuringly. 'If you want me to come, no one will keep me out.'

In the afternoon, Paris took part in a general drill with his fellow-gladiators. Blue shadows of evening had flooded the high-walled palaestra with the under-sea gloom Paris had noticed on his first visit. When he returned to his cell he fell face downwards on the hard mattress and into a deep sleep.

He was shaken awake by a pair of slaves who had brought water for him to bathe. It felt as though he had been asleep for a long time, but, when he asked the hour, he was surprised to hear that it was still early evening. The young gladiator asked them the reason for the change of routine: usually he bathed after his evening meal.

The slaves exchanged a conspiratorial smile. 'Tonight you will be dining in Corax's chambers,' one of them explained. They had brought him a fine silk tunic of cornflower blue, and a new pair of sandals, studded with silver. This could only mean a session with one of the gladiators, thought Paris. Why tonight, when he felt close to despair? He needed to be with Publius, to tell his troubles, ask the soldier's advice and draw on his strength.

Two guards arrived and marched him off along the portico with ringing steps. The gladiators were constantly grumbling how Corax had grown wealthy on their blood. He had a fine villa in the city, but he also kept an apartment within the school for receiving clients. Few of the gladiators had ever set foot there, but rumours circulated about the richness of its decoration and furnishings.

It was months since Paris had been in gracious surroundings. He was led to a chamber on the upper floor of the building. As the guards closed the door discreetly behind him, The young man was dazzled for a moment by thousands of tiny flames dancing on the branches of tall bronze candelabra and the brilliant reds and blues of the frescos which covered the walls. Points of gold glinted among the rich mosaic patterns of the floor. It took a moment before Paris' eyes wandered to the table, already set with a feast on finely worked silver plates.

To his astonishment, the only other occupant of the room, already reclining on a couch by the table, was not, as he expected, a gladiator, but his friend Publius.

The soldier gave a delighted laugh at Paris' reaction. 'Come,' he called, patting the couch. 'Gladiators in training need to eat.'

'But how did you manage this?' asked Paris, as Publius poured wine into silver goblets. For the first time, he was seeing his friend out of uniform. He looked younger, boyish even in a simple white tunic trimmed with purple, though he was perhaps ten years older than Paris. His height made him appear lean, but Paris noticed that the soldier's legs and arms were chiselled with hard muscle, the result of forced marches carrying heavy equipment.

'If you mean how did I persuade Corax to let me have this room - and you - for the night. That was simple. We soldiers are essential to the functioning of the amphitheatre - so relations with the school are good. If, on the other hand, you mean how can an ordinary soldier like me afford to provide a decent supper for a friend' - his eyes twinkled under thick eyebrows - 'well, I am not quite an ordinary soldier. Are you aware that the Urban Cohorts are affiliated to the Praetorian Guards?'

'The Emperor's own bodyguard,' commented Paris, impressed.

'Yes,' confirmed Publius, pleased at the young man's reaction. 'And we receive more than three times the pay of an ordinary legionary. The Emperor feeds and clothes us: so I have managed to put a little aside for when I might need it. This is just such an occasion,' he smiled.

The soldier went on to explain how he had fought under Vespasian in the civil war in which he had received medals for saving the lives of his fellow legionaries. His valour had come to the attention of the tribune of his legion and he had been rewarded with a transfer to the Urban Cohorts. From there it would be but a short step to the Praetorian Guard, the Empire's military elite. That would also mean a rise in pay, he quickly pointed out. Paris was touched. He realised that the other man was formally presenting his credentials - like a suitor.

He on the other hand, as far Publius was concerned, had little to recommend him. He was that most wretched of slaves - a gladiator. Why should Publius be interested in him? Yet the elaborate arrangements he had made for their evening together proved that he was.

In Publius' company, Paris felt himself more at ease than he had for months, maybe years. Earlier in the day, he had longed to meet with his friend in order to unburden himself. Now his problems seemed to have faded by themselves in the warmth of companionship. He found himself gripped by Publius' account of his military achievements and future plans. It was completely without vanity: Publius was at pains to stress not his military glory but his good financial prospects and
Paris was charmed by the soldier's eagerness to make a good impression.

'But we're not here to talk about me,' said Publius gently, having said his piece. He turned on his side to face Paris and took him by the hand. 'I knew that there was something wrong today at the practice - and I can still see it in your eyes now. You have the look of a man who has lost his way. A man who has lost hope. Yet from the first moment I saw you, even though you were a slave, I felt you were someone who knew where he was going. What went wrong, my little gladiator?'

Paris began to tell his story, hesitantly at first, from the time he escaped from his uncle's farm. The other man listened so intently, that the words soon began to pour from him. Publius seemed to live every detail, frowning at the ill-treatment meted out to Paris by his uncle, nodding with approval at the daring of the young man's flight, laughing at the descriptions of his narrow escapes from the stewards of country estates.

When Paris described his experiences in Diogenes' household and his subsequent sale to Corax, however, he noticed Publius flush with anger. At the point when Paris revealed how Lucius had taken his documents and Diogenes had destroyed them, the soldier could contain himself no longer. 'These are evil men and deserve to be punished. The decree of freedom comes from the Emperor himself. To defy that decree is to oppose the divine Caesar: it is a sacrilege.'

Suddenly his tone of anger turned to one of concern. And he touched Paris' cheek. 'But I hate them most of all because they hurt you, Paris.'

When Paris went on to talk of his feelings of despair, following the news that his hopes for immediate freedom had been crushed, he glimpsed for the first time Publius the soldier, a man disciplined with himself and others. His expression became almost stern.

'Paris, don't talk this way. Of course, it will take longer for you to win your freedom as a gladiator. And you will face constant danger. But much less than a soldier must confront in battle. Corax has faith in you. You are valuable to him and he will not put your life in unnecessary danger. I have faith in you too. And I will do everything in my power to help.'

Publius stared searchingly at Paris. He still held the young man's hand firmly in his. 'So now you are free of your attachment to Lucius?'

Paris flushed lightly. 'I never want to see him again.' He smiled briefly at the soldier, then glanced down at the couch. He felt strangely nervous. His feelings for Publius welled up inside him.

But he knew that he would have to make the first move - or at least hint that he was willing. He knew that, for all his bravado, the older man would never force his attentions on another: he was far too correct for that.

How different to the approaches he had become used to over the past few months thought Paris, wryly.

'A few days ago,' said Paris, still staring down at the couch, 'you said you wanted to kiss me, if a mortal was allowed to kiss a god.' He looked up at Publius: 'Well I'm not a god. I am mortal just like you.'

Paris was astonished at Publius' response. He seized the young man in his arms and frantically covered his face with kisses. He plunged his tongue into Paris' open mouth. The cool, rather proper soldier, was suddenly possessed by a fury of passion. Never ceasing to explore Paris' mouth, Publius undid the young man's loincloth with urgent fumblings. He broke the embrace for a split second as he pulled off Paris' tunic. Snatching another violent kiss, he sat up abruptly to rip off his own tunic. A flush coloured the soldier's face and neck, almost reaching down to his chest.

Now they were both naked, Publius rolled Paris on to his back. With a sudden movement, he shifted position, threw Paris' legs against his shoulders and began furiously lapping at the boy's anus. He spat a blob of saliva on the pink button and stared at it hard for a split second as though trying to impress every tiny wrinkle on his memory, before attacking the lubricated hole with long hungry strokes of his tongue. Caught up in the urgency of Publius' passion, Paris rocked his hips in reply: immediately the soldier held his head immobile so that the young man's slowly unfolding pucker ground against his tongue.

Raising his head slightly, Publius took Paris' heavy balls in his mouth, first one, then, with a slight struggle, both. They were already pulled tight with arousal into Paris' crotch. As Publius tugged with a steady pressure, he could see just beyond his nose, the young man's proud white column, stiff and straight, straining upwards from his flat stomach. Publius' eyes widened at this first glimpse of his lover's manhood. He instantly released the boy's testicles and devoured the entire length of Paris' rod with one rapid swallow.

Paris groaned. He pressed his heels against Publius firm back, levering his cock even deeper into the soldier's throat.

Publius pulled his mouth from Paris' burning rod and brought his face close to the young man's. He wore an anxious expression. 'What are your other names? I only know you as Paris. I am Publius Valerius Arrianus.

And you?' He stared at Paris with anxious expectancy.

Paris could not suppress a smile that Publius should choose such a moment for a formal introduction. 'Livius Metilius Paris,' he replied and, as though responding to a passionate declaration of love, Publius kissed him savagely. The soldier sucked hard on the boy's tongue and chewed at Paris' lips until they were stained red, like those of a child who has gorged on berries.

At the same time, Publius was pushing Paris knees back with a powerful grip. Paris could feel movement and pressure against his ass and was suddenly aware of a feeling of fullness in his rectum. Publius had entered him with such gentleness and skill that there had been no pain and now there was only pleasure as the older man began to fuck him with hypnotic strokes. Sometimes he would pull all the way back, teasing Paris' sphincter with his shiny glans, stretching it with tantalising circular movements. Whenever he did this, Publius would break off their kisses for a moment, so that he could study his lover's face and observe the pleasure that clouded Paris' eyes with every twist of the soldier's cockhead. The pleasure mounted exquisitely, as the two men led each other from one plateau of delight to another.

Eventually, with a sob of pleasure, Publius could bear it no longer. Never breaking his gaze from that of Paris, he gritted his teeth and began to ram his cock into his lover's vitals with all the strength he could muster. The veins stood out on the soldier's forehead as he sent a shudder through Paris' body with every hammer-blow. The soldier's rhythmic groans became a single long roar as a tidal wave in his loins carried him inexorably to climax. Publius' back arched and his head and limbs jerked like one in a seizure, his eyes and mouth narrowed to slits as the spasms of pleasure wracked his whole body. Paris's member, red-raw and glossy with extended stimulation, stood erect. With a final shudder it paused for an instant before criss-crossing the smooth plane of Publius' stomach with strings of seminal fluid.

Publius collapsed across Paris' body and lay there motionless for some minutes. Paris gently cupped the cropped head in his hands, caressing it softly. Abruptly, the soldier began to kiss the young man with renewed passion, as though for the first time that night. He pushed down on Paris' shoulders until the boy's head reached his loins and then, raising his hips, steered Paris' lips to his anus.

Publius' sturdy member was already erect. Tears of love-juice poured, one after another, from his slit, forming a film over his exposed glans, as Paris' tongue slid in endless circles over his asshole. The soldier's anus was of the palest pink, almost white, and nearly flat, with long wrinkles stretched out tautly all around it in a perfect circle. Their eyes were locked over Publius' balls.

'Take me,' hissed Publius forcefully. 'I want you inside me, Paris. I want to carry your essence away in my body.'

Paris did not need any urging and scrambled towards Publius' face, stabbing his mouth with his tongue. At the same time, with his cock, he prodded the soldier's silken, hairless hole, already slippery with spittle. Paris inhaled deeply on his lover's smell: a sweet-sour masculine mix of wine, perfume and sweat. Intoxicated, the boy could not help thrusting with some violence in his desperation to probe the other man's body with his fuckpole. Publius responded with equally powerful thrusts of his pelvis in his longing to be impaled on the boy's throbbing meat. The soldier gave a long sigh of satisfaction as their opposing forces met and Paris' cock sank all the way into his entrails.

'Fuck me Paris. Plant your seed in my hole,' begged Publius, as he pushed hard against Paris' stiff staff. 'Run me through with your sword, little gladiator,' he begged. 'Pierce my guts with your weapon, just as you have pierced my heart with your beauty.'

Once more, Paris felt himself swept along on the wild current of Publius' passion. The soldier's hole held the young man's cock in a firm grasp, friction building with each stroke. 'I'm going to come,' Paris cried, his eyes wide with surprise.

'Yes, come now, fill me with your seed,' Publius ordered sharply, an expression of stern determination on his face as he stared hard into Paris' eyes. The young man could feel Publius' fuckhole contracting around his rod like a hungry mouth ready to suck out his load. 'Yes,' cried Paris urgently. 'I'm shooting.' The contractions were strong and slow with a long pause between each. Publius eyes were closed and his head flung back. He jerked his ass violently as if to gobble every last drop of Paris' love-liquid. Without a sound, his lips pursed, Publius arched his head up from the bed. His beefy prick rose and fell repeatedly, flinging long thin streams of white semen over the silken black hair which patterned his chest and abdomen.

Paris stretched lazily on the couch. They had not slept a wink - and he had a day's hard training before him. But he did not feel tired. On the contrary he was filled with energy and optimism. He turned to Publius, leaning his head on his elbow. Publius lay on his back, a smile playing about his lips. Paris gently traced the fine, proud mouth with his fingertips. 'Perhaps I am a god after all,' murmured the young man. 'Or at least, you have made me feel like one.'

Paris walked out of the chamber and across the balcony, overlooking the palaestra. Pink shreds of cloud drifted in the washed-out morning sky. Pillars and gilded roofs of temples, rosy in the sun's rays, could be glimpsed rising beyond the grim walls of the school. It seemed an age since Paris had entered the chamber. Now he no longer felt alone. The young gladiator gazed down at the empty rectangle of the palaestra. Till now, it had always felt like the drill yard of a prison: now it stretched before him like the path to freedom.

At the end of the summer, with the games' season almost over for the year Paris' life had taken on a new and purposeful pattern. Almost every night was spent with Publius, usually at the school, although on some occasions, Corax invited them to his villa or gave Paris permission to visit Publius at his barracks. The soldier had been appointed optio, second in command to his centurion, which meant more spacious quarters and - he was quick to point out - higher wages.

Publius' devotion filled Paris with awe. Even though freedom was still a far-off dream, he felt safe and contented whenever he was in the other man's company. Publius made a sacrifice at the temple of Fortuna, goddess of destiny, on behalf of them both. 'I prayed for your future freedom and our future together,' he explained. The augurers of the goddess had predicted glory for both men. What could that mean, they wondered excitedly?

By day, however, he saw another side to the soldier. Most of the week, Paris would train at the school, but now he was permitted to go once or twice a week with the other gladiators to the large palaestra next to the amphitheatre.

As well as following the official training programme of the school, Publius had agreed with Corax that Paris would carry out additional exercises which the soldier himself would supervise. Paris found this military drill far more gruelling than Corax's - and Publius was a hard task-master.

One exercise consisted of running fifty laps round the large palaestra while weighed down with the armour and baggage of a foot-soldier in the Roman army. The other gladiators would roar with laughter as they watched Paris panting round the course. When the young gladiator sank to his knees at the end of one of these marathons, Publius would shrug and casually comment: 'That's nothing: when I was in the legion we would sometimes be forced to cover thirty miles a day with a far heavier load than that - and then fight a battle.' Paris stared up at him, too out of breath to reply.

After some months of this training, Paris found that his armour and weapons felt as light as silk.

Another exercise Publius devised was to make Paris take on two opponents at once - usually one of the gladiators and himself. The first time they attempted this, Paris was taken aback at the ferocity with which his lover attacked him. At the end of the bout, Publius showed little sympathy. 'In battle, you are attacked from all sides. True, you can hope that your companions will look out for you, but you cannot ask the enemy to wait while you fight them in turn. If you are able to parry the blows of two assailants at once, you will acquire a speed and vigilance that a single man will be unable to match.'

As Paris became more skilled at this exercise - and neither his gladiator partner nor his lover gave him any quarter - the other gladiators would often gather silently around him, watching the young man skilfully fend off his attackers and wondering if this could be the same youth who had played Apollo so prettily at the previous summer's games.

That winter the two men preferred to spend the evenings in Publius' quarters as they were furnished with a bronze brazier and were far cosier than Paris' bare cell. One chilly evening in February, they had just made love by the orange glow from the open door of the brazier. Publius sat up on the bed and looked down admiringly at Paris' naked body. 'Who would have imagined that the lad I met all those months ago would have changed so fast.' He ran his hand over the square slabs of Paris' chest and down the small neat rectangles of his abdomen. He stroked the hard, powerful thighs and chiselled calves, the wide shoulders and bulging arms. Even the face had taken on the angularity of manhood. 'You have become a man and, more than that, a gladiator.'

'Thanks to you,' said Paris, sleepily, reaching up to stroke his lover's cheek. 'There is only one way I can show my gratitude: by becoming a champion. And I will. I promise you.'

Paris was due to make his debut in the amphitheatre in the course of the April games. Corax was determined to make the most of his young protege and decided that he would be pitted against Niceros. Known to audiences as the Bear because of his hairy body and enormous height and bulk, the veteran fighter played a villain in the ring. After felling his opponent, he would stride around the arena roaring abuse at the crowd.

Some of them would respond with good-humoured banter while others would work themselves into such a frenzy that their friends would have to restrain them from throwing themselves headfirst into the ring - where, no doubt, Niceros would have made short work of them.

He would be the perfect match for the young hero, the fair Apollo, Corax had decided. Although Paris' face would be completely covered by his helmet, the rumours would soon go round the crowd that he was none other than the beautiful boy who stole their hearts the previous summer. Of course, the fight would be carefully rehearsed to give the victory to Niceros. The crowd would be sure to call for the youngster to be spared - and anyway the editor of the games would be instructed to decide in his favour.

Eager to prove himself after a hard winter's training, Paris was galled at the idea that he would be forced to lose. But the important thing was to make a name for himself. And anyway, what newcomer in his first combat could expect to defeat the mighty Niceros?

The older gladiator was sullen during the rehearsals for the contest: he resented the fact that he no longer had access to Paris' services.

On the morning of the fight, Publius burnt incense at the Temple of Fortuna. As he reported for duty at the amphitheatre, a dove fluttered down from a pine tree and perched on his shoulder – surely a good omen, he assured Paris when they met. Later Paris was to be glad of that knowl-

Ben Elliott

edge.

Paris knew that it was vital not to succumb to nerves. When Publius was able, he slipped down to the corridors under the stands and they chatted about unimportant matters in order to keep the young gladiator's mind off the forthcoming combat. Part of the time, however, Paris spent exercising and running through the sequence of the fight in his mind: although some of the bout would be spontaneous, it would follow a pre-planned order in which both fighters would be allowed moments of glory, though Niceros would be the ultimate victor.

Publius made a final check of his lover's armour as the moment of the fight approached, locking his helmet in position. As Paris bade farewell to the soldier, he was struck by a terrible thought: what if the fight did not go according to plan? He stared through his visor at the strong face he had grown to love and trust. He quickly put the idea out of his mind: if his resolve failed now, he was lost. Fortunately, Publius had received permission from his centurion to be present in the ring and would be advising Paris during the contest.

Corax would be coaching Niceros: it was a standing joke at the school that without the lanista's help the hulking gladiator would not even know which way to face.

Paris felt his heart pounding as he took the gladiator's oath for the first time: 'I will give myself up to be flogged, burned or put to the sword if I disobey.' The smell of red-hot metal reminded him that these were not just words and that those who did falter in the ring – usually criminals rather than professional gladiators - really would be goaded by hot irons and whips.

Tumultuous applause broke out as Paris stepped into the arena. The news had gone round like wildfire that the fighter billed as Apollo was indeed the lad they had cheered so soundly the previous year. Paris saw his opponent approaching from the other side of the arena. He was swearing at the crowd and making obscene gestures with his sword. Niceros fought as a Thracian, which meant that his face was also concealed by a helmet. But, as he gesticulated furiously, he appeared to be genuinely riled by the crowd's enthusiastic support for Paris.

The two gladiators circled one another, as they had rehearsed, Paris with his long rectangular shield and scimitar and the Thracian with his short curved dagger and small round shield of bronze. The crowd fell silent, deep in concentration. Paris abruptly changed direction and when Niceros mirrored his manoeuvre, headed directly for him. They engaged in a brief flurry of flashy moves, then broke apart, each acknowledging the applause on opposite sides of the arena.

Paris could hear Niceros' powerful voice bellowing abuse at the crowd. They gave as good as they got. The supporters of Apollo raised their chant once more and it was taken up by the entire throng.

Paris turned round, ready to launch into the next stage of the match. But something was wrong. The two men were supposed to dodge each other with zig-zag moves. Niceros, however, was hurtling directly towards him at an alarming speed. Paris hesitated a moment, unsure how to react. Suddenly the chant petered out. Niceros was almost upon him. The crowd sensed Paris' disorientation.

Paris kept his eye on the Thracian's flashing dagger, his shield at the ready. The approaching gladiator vanished in a blinding flash of light. Followed by a moment of blackness. Something struck Paris' helmet with a sickening crash and the cries of the mob were drowned by a ringing in his ears. The amphitheatre had turned upside down. The sandy arena was jammed against his helmet like a sloping ceiling. Was that the sky below him or the sea? The crowd appeared to fall from their seats in unison as though they were about to dive headfirst into the deep blue expanse. But they stopped suddenly, hanging by their feet. Now Niceros was dangling in the sky right next to him, his dagger raised and his polished shield shining like a second sun.

More by instinct than design, Paris slipped his shield from his arm and, holding it at one end, rammed it into Niceros' bulging crotch as hard as he could. Although he was still not sure what was up and what was down, there was no mistaking where that was. The audience threw their arms in the air, cheering, as Niceros doubled up. Using the shield as a support, Paris hauled himself to his feet. Fortunately, he had clung to his sword throughout the incident.

Maddened by the pain, Niceros began to lash out wildly with his dagger. Paris managed to parry the blows with his shield, rhythmically interspersing these moves with thrusts of his sword. Niceros, however, with his greater height and strength, tossed these strokes aside with his bronze shield as though Paris was attacking him with a palm frond.

The taller man began to push his opponent back towards the arena wall. Paris could feel its presence behind him: it was so close that he could pick out the cries of advice from spectators leaning over the parapet. 'Go for his neck, Apollo!' 'Give him another one in the balls!'

Judging the distance from these calls, Paris leapt back against the wall just as Niceros was lunging at him with his dagger, forcing the taller man to lean forward, throwing him off-balance. But the dagger struck cold marble with a shower of sparks. Paris was not there. Sliding down the wall, he had dodged behind Niceros and, taking advantage of his opponent's momentary loss of equilibrium, whacked him across the head and back with his rectangular shield as hard as he could. Niceros had laid the ground-rules when he had used his shield to dazzle the younger gladiator: in this match there were no rules.

Now Niceros fell forward, striking his head against the wall. His legs were buckling and Paris brought the edge of his shield hard against the crook of Niceros' knees, felling the giant with a blow. The hand in which Niceros held his dagger had slipped to the ground. Paris stamped hard on his fingers, forcing them to open, and snatched the dagger away.

Dazed, his face pressed to the wall of the arena, Niceros froze as the cold metal of Paris' sword slid under his chin. He threw a tentative glance backwards and the horrible realisation could be seen in his eyes: for the first time he had lost a fight. And to this inexperienced newcomer - this pretty boy who was good for one thing only.

The mob was calling for blood, shaking their thumbs vigorously to express their wishes to the editor. Though his heart was dancing to a crazy rhythm, Paris maintained a calm demeanour. He looked towards the editor's box and awaited the command. He knew that Corax would not want one of his leading gladiators killed, and also that the editor would not want to pay the steep additional fee involved. Sure enough, the editor raised his closed fist which meant that Niceros was to be spared.

Paris slowly backed off, still holding his sword and Niceros' dagger. As cries of 'Up with Apollo' echoed around the auditorium, Niceros stumbled to the nearest exit and disappeared from view. His reputation in the arena of Pompeii was in ruins.

There was a banquet that night at the school and Corax proposed a toast to Paris. He threw a grim glance towards Niceros, staring sullenly into his wine at the end of one of the long tables. On their return from the amphitheatre that evening, Corax had summoned Niceros to his chambers, and everyone had listened nervously as the lanista's angry words rang out across the palaestra. Disobedience would not be tolerated in the school. One more performance like that and Niceros would be packed off to the salt mines, the lanista had told him.

Most of the gladiators were delighted at Paris' success. He was their good-luck charm: if Apollo the gladiator was victorious, surely the gods smiled on the school. Like a proud parent, Thrax beamed down the table at the young gladiator. All Paris could think of, however, was the prize money: he was on his way to purchasing his freedom. There had been no time for him and Publius to celebrate at the arena and tonight the soldier was on duty. Tomorrow they would have their own private victory celebration. The one that mattered. The dream they shared was a little closer.

Late that night, Paris was awoken by the grating of a key turning slowly in the lock. Half-asleep, he thought it might be Publius, but then he remembered that his lover was working till dawn. As the door flew open, several burly figures, outlined by moonlight tumbled into the room. Paris sat bolt upright, but before he could call out, the figures fell on him.

A meaty paw was clenched over his mouth as his hands and feet were tied together. Brawny arms lifted him from the bed as though he were a feather pillow. Although he could see no faces, he could tell from their physiques that these men were gladiators - there seemed to be a group of four or five. Paris' struggles were fruitless as they hurried stealthily along the portico, holding him pinned under their arms like a rolled-up carpet.

They turned into a lighted doorway. The door closed behind them with a soft boom and Paris was tossed onto the floor. Looking up, he saw Niceros towering over him and, raising his head from the floor with some difficulty, Paris realised they were in the Thracian's apartment. As a champion, he had special privileges, including this suite of finely decorated and furnished rooms. The other men grouped around Niceros and Paris could now see that there were indeed five of them.

Niceros said nothing. He was naked except for a short belted kilt which he now slipped down over his hips and kicked to one side. His fleshy weapon swayed menacingly, magnified by Paris' floor-level view.

Ben Elliott

The thick foreskin was already retreating from the crimson glans. The other gladiators, exchanging knowing leers, followed Niceros' example and stripped off their kilts and tunics. They began to stroke their low-slung members. Paris noted with alarm that Niceros' rod was starting to stiffen and rise, although, even when flaccid it, was the shape and size of a large cucumber.

'This is what we do to those who betray their fellow gladiators,' growled Niceros. He grabbed Paris long blond tresses and pulled him to his knees. Jerking the young gladiator's head back, he made a gesture to another of the men. With a broad smile, revealing rows of rotten teeth, the other man, whom Paris recognised as Rodan, another Thracian, prised Paris' mouth open with both hands, as a bestiarius would a tiger. Paris saw Niceros' half-erect member swaying towards his face. He was surprised when Niceros positioned the tip just above his open mouth and held it there.

'I've got a lot of wine to get rid of, boys,' Niceros roared over his shoulder. 'How about you?'

'Barrels of it, Niceros,' retorted Rodan.

He turned back to Paris. The hairy giant screwed up his face with effort and, as he emitted an incoherent grunt, a broad stream of piss gushed from his slit into the young gladiator's unsuspecting mouth. Paris struggled, choking and gagging on the warm golden liquid. Fleetingly, he registered the fact that the man's urine was completely tasteless - he had expected it to be salty. But Niceros tugged hard on his hair and Rodan held his jaws firmly apart. He found himself instinctively swallowing - it was that or drown in Niceros' piss.

The other men crowded round eagerly. Niceros cut off the powerful jet and another man stepped into his place. A foaming stream shot into Paris' mouth and he gulped desperately to keep pace with the flow. Niceros had disappeared from Paris' view. Preoccupied with swallowing the gladiator's seemingly endless stream, Paris could not keep track of the rapid changes that were happening around him. Powerful hands were pulling him to his feet, though others forced him to remain bent forward, glugging on the human spring.

Paris' tunic was torn roughly from his body. Something began to thud dully against his anus. In the confusion of the moment, it reminded

Paris of the bass drum in the arena, but this drumstick struck with a sound-less beat. Abruptly, the thumping became a single constant force. This could only be Niceros, thought Paris, in panic, as his sphincter was trans-formed into a blazing ring of red-hot metal.

Incredibly, the gladiator was still emptying his bladder down Paris' gullet, while another was pointing his cock ominously in Paris' face. A blinding fountain of piss stung the young man's eyes. The man waved his appendage from side to side, drenching Paris' face and hair.

Meanwhile the searing pain in his hole continued, as Niceros contin-ued to spear his gut. Suddenly the powerful gladiator stopped thrusting. Paris tried to turn. 'Keep still,' Niceros boomed and two of the others held Paris' legs immobile. Nothing seemed to be happening. The two men who had been pissing in his face and mouth seemed to have exhausted their supply, at least for the moment, and their cocks dripped, semi-erect in Paris' face. All the men seemed to be holding their breath. Then Niceros exhaled so strongly that Paris felt the hot gust on his shoulders. Still noth-ing seemed to happen.

Slowly, Paris felt a fullness building in his bowels and an urgent need to empty them. Niceros moaned and began to push again. His cock seemed to move smoothly as though riding on copious amounts of lubrication. As the Thracian increased his rhythm, Paris could feel rivulets running from his anus and down his legs. Then it hit him: Niceros had pissed in his arse. The man was now fucking the young gladiator franti-cally, his cock sloshing in his own urine.

By now, the other men were enraged with animal lust. One was pumping Paris' mouth with his veined purple column, while another was relieving himself with broad sweeps of piss over the young gladiator's back. As Niceros' unplugged Paris' hole, unleashing a hot stream of fluid, a third man immediately dammed the flow with his own hard manhood and began to fuck powerfully with the full length of his pole.

Rodan, with a sigh of relief, directed the results of the night's drink-ing on the spot where the cock entered Paris' ass. Squinting up from the appendage wedged down his throat, Paris glimpsed Niceros, his lips twist-ed in a grim smile. He was holding a massive dildo - which seemed to Paris a similacrum of the Thracian's own towering manhood immortalised in bronze. The gladiator's huge paws were smearing it with some kind of ointment. With a grin, he held the fearsome instrument close to Paris' face. A pungent, spicy smell pricked his nostrils.

Niceros disappeared, and Paris felt a long withdrawal from his guts. No sooner had the cock pulled out, however, than pain jolted his entire frame. It was as though the metal rod thrust into his vitals was attracting lightning bolts from the heavens. It was not just that his rectum was being stretched far beyond its capacity: he had already felt that with Niceros. Now, it was as though the lining of his gut had caught fire as the hard metal of the dildo plunged in and out of his well-lubricated hole.

'Recognise that boy? You should. I once fucked an artist. "Future generations must share this delight," he told me. So he cast my prick in bronze. Like it?'

Paris, his mouth stopped up by a gladiator's cock could only grunt painfully.

'I smeared it with a love-ointment I got from a witch. I'm not as mean as you think. I want you to enjoy what's coming to you, boy.'

Seeing Paris writhe in agony as Niceros twisted and jerked the dildo in the young man's inflamed hole, the other gladiators were spurred to inflict more pain and began to whack Paris' buttocks with the flat of their callused palms and beat his white back with leather thongs.

Using the dildo as a rudder Niceros steered Paris brutally across the room, pushing him forward over the edge of an ornate bronze couch. Pulling the rigid weapon roughly from Paris' arse, the older gladiator shoved his own into the gaping scarlet hole, right up to the hilt.

Paris heard gruff whispers exchanged behind him as the others huddled close. Although Niceros' member was buried deep in Paris' insides, he was not thrusting. Suddenly the veteran gladiator straightened his powerful legs, lifting Paris off the bed, supported on the huge tool. Niceros slowly turned, holding Paris in position, and sat on the edge of the couch. Paris now faced the other gladiators. In this position, Niceros' column seemed to penetrate still further.

The four other men, their eyes feasting on the sight of Niceros' swollen member pumping Paris' arse, were furiously massaging their own not inconsiderable erections. Niceros lay back on the couch, pulling Paris down on top of him. One of the other men was fingering Paris' asshole. At first the young man thought they were just exploring the action of Niceros rod. But, staring hard at Paris, the man spat in his palm and rubbed his ruby glans. He leaned towards Paris, pushing the young man's legs back and up. Paris caught a whiff of his wine-soaked breath and felt the man's cock bob softly against the knife edge tautness of his anus. Then a bolt of pain shot through Paris' violated hole. To his horror, he realised that a second cock was about to enter him.

Double-penetration by two outsize organs provoked such torment that Paris blacked out. When he emerged from his faint, he gazed into the red faced and bulging eyes of another man, fucking him frenziedly.

Supporting Paris' arse with his strong hands, Niceros was raising and lowering the young man on his thick pole, so that he was being vigorously fucked by two cocks at once, and at different speeds. With savage bellows, the second gladiator came, and as he withdrew exhausted, Rodan stepped eagerly into his place, his rotten teeth bared in a ghoulish grin.

Niceros' revenge was to double-fuck the victor with each of the men in turn. Paris tried to switch off his thoughts and simply wait for the ordeal to end.

As the last man reached his climax, injecting yet another thick load into the mingled man-cream which already greased Paris' guts, Niceros moved his hands to Paris hips ramming the man's ass hard against his pelvis. Paris recognised the low groan that stared in Niceros belly and grew in volume until it shook the bronze couch. Trumpeting like an elephant, Niceros came, his hefty frame thrusting under Paris so strongly that the young man almost bounced off the end of his pillar.

The intensity of the feeling in his bowels and the sight of the other gladiators, furiously jerking their members, wide-eyed as goldfish, pushed Paris over the edge. Almost as though it belonged to someone else, he watched his own dick leap and quiver as it erupted in white spurts of ball-juice. At this, the other gladiators jostled against him, hosing him down with hot springs of cum.

It was still dark when the gladiators dumped Paris, naked and face down, in the centre of the palaestra. Niceros wanted this incident to serve as a warning to others that his supremacy in the arena was not to be chal-

Ben Elliott

lenged.

Paris tried to crawl across the sand to his cell, but the pain overcame him as he moved and he lost consciousness. A cold breeze blew just before dawn. Footsteps padded across the sand. There was hard breathing like a bull as it eyes the fighter. Strong arms scooped Paris effortlessly from the ground and carried him back to his cell. Between sleep and waking, Paris felt large hands wash him gently and smear his damaged anus with soothing ointment before covering him with a soft counterpane that was not his. He fell asleep until daybreak.

For a moment he was not sure what had woken him - the sun streaming through the open door of his cell or the gruff voices of the gladiators raised in excitement. He managed to raise himself from the bed and staggered stiffly towards the door. The entire population of the school was gathered around the exercise equipment at the far end of the palaestra. Corax was striding towards the group, accompanied by guards. Silence fell, broken only by a high pitched sqeaking of metal on metal. As the gladiators parted to let Corax pass, Paris saw clearly the cause of the excitement.

Niceros' massive frame, stripped stark naked, had been lashed to one of the revolving wooden practice figures, his face pressed to the wooden face of the effigy. His legs were streaked with dried blood and a dark brown shadow showed where it had sunk into the sand. Protruding from his asshole was his own sword, embedded to the hilt. The figure squeaked as it swung slowly back and forth.

When Paris' own injuries came to light - they prevented him from fighting for some days - Corax launched an immediate investigation and the four surviving attackers were jailed in the school's own cramped prison cells. The guards who had been bribed to hand over the keys to Paris cell were dismissed. The lanista was furious that his plans for Paris had been temporarily thwarted. He did not even bother to investigate the slaying of Niceros.

The moment the news of Niceros' attack on Paris reached Publius, the soldier was by his lover's side. He was granted leave to watch over the boy day and night. But the young gladiator made a swift recovery and within the week Paris was back in the arena.

At the end of an afternoon's combat, having received his prize money, he was peeling off his armour in a dressing room. Thrax entered and congratulated his young colleague on his latest win. He punched Paris playfully on the shoulder, his weather-beaten face cracking into a sheepish grin.

The elder gladiator looked round to check that no one was near and then leaning close to Paris said in a husky whisper, 'We showed him, boy, didn't we?'

CHAPTER 7

Pale early morning sunlight slanted through the pines that clustered around the main palaestra of Pompeii, casting long diagonal shadows across the smooth golden sand. Even though it was only the first hour of the day, the square was humming with activity as the gladiators prepared for their exercises. The May morning was pleasantly warm. Paris was sitting on the step of the portico polishing his helmet, when he was suddenly aware of a silent presence beside him. He held up his arm against the low sun, and could not hide a look of surprise when he saw Lucius staring down at him.

Paris immediately glanced away, colouring slightly, and began to rub furiously at his helmet. 'Congratulations on your victories,' said Lucius quietly. 'I've been attending the games over the past few days since I got back.'

Following Paris' combat with Niceros, and the crowd's reaction, Corax had decided that the new gladiator should enjoy a few wins and the May games were proving a triumph for him.

'I'm here alone,' Lucius continued. 'My father hasn't returned for the summer yet. The villa's still closed up and I'm staying at an inn.'

Breathing hard on his helmet, Paris continued polishing as though he had not heard a word.

'I have renounced all links with him, Paris. I am disinherited. We have hardly spoken to one another since I last met you. I will never forgive him for coming between us. Not that I'm trying to excuse my own part in the matter, of course,' he added hurriedly, with a blush

'I really don't care about any of this,' Paris interrupted in an irritated tone. 'My life has changed for the better, and I'd rather forget what happened.'

'We're going to be seeing a lot of each other now. I thought you should know. And I'd rather you heard it from me,' Lucius explained. 'What other choice does a ruined rich boy have than to become a gladiator? Corax has accepted me for training as a retiarius. I have renounced my rights as a citizen: from now on, my will is subject to the school, just as yours is.'

The young gladiator cast a brief professional glance at Lucius: with his tall lean physique, and his training as a knight, he would handle a net and trident with skill. And Paris had to acknowledge that he would cut a fine figure in the arena.

'Of course, I am still a citizen so I won't be living at the school. But I will train every day. Corax wants me to be ready for next year's games.'

'Bit of a come-down for the aedile's son, isn't it?' Paris' voice was tinged with sarcasm and a half-smile played on his lips.

'That's just it,' replied Lucius: 'my father's known here, so I reckoned that people would come to watch me fight out of sheer evil curiosity. Nothing pleases the public more than to see the powerful brought low.'

'Won't it be rather embarrassing for your father.'

'Absolutely,' replied Lucius, flashing the winning smile Paris knew so well.

Paris felt something stirring inside him and quickly suppressed it.

'I told you when we parted,' he said in a flat tone, strapping on his leg-armour with deep concentration, 'that we would meet again as strangers. Nothing has changed for me,' he turned sharply to his former lover: 'You should also know, Lucius, that I have someone else. I owe him my life.' Paris saw Lucius flinch at his words. He went back to adjusting the straps.

'You may not care to hear it now, but I want you to know that I've changed because of you and because of what we had - and lost,' said Lucius. 'Breaking with my father, joining the school: it's the start of a new life for me. I hope to become the kind of man you wanted me to be.'

Paris made no answer. Sliding the blank mask of the helmet over his head, he scooped up his sword and shield and walked away.

Although they saw each other daily during training sessions at the school or in the large palaestra, Paris studiously ignored Lucius. But the gladiator would often be aware of the other man's large dark eyes fixed on him while he exercised or fought a partner with dummy weapons. Paris was particularly conscious of Lucius' searching gaze whenever Publius was present. The young man considered his training far from complete and still relied on the soldier for advice and coaching.

Following his acclaim at the May games, the reputation of Apollo the gladiator began to spread throughout the region of Campania. Corax received invitations to send a team of his fighters to games at nearby Nola or Puteoli - on condition that the celebrated Apollo was among them. Not all of Paris' bouts were rigged: several times he had the satisfaction of winning by skill alone. On a few occasions the crowd became so maddened in their enthusiasm for Apollo that they shook their thumbs in the gesture that meant death for his opponent - and the editor was forced to concede to their wishes. At first it was distasteful for the inexperienced gladiator to deliver the ritualised coup de grace in cold blood, watching his adversary staring up at him, patiently baring his breast for the final blow. But he soon learned to complete the deed swiftly and cleanly, without emotion. The crowds, on the other hand, became delirious at the sight of the crimson flood.

By the end of Pompeii's Apollo games in July, Paris had chalked up ten victories in a single season - an unheard of achievement: many successful gladiators could not boast more than twenty wins in an entire career. Paris was beginning to enjoy the adulation that went with his success. But far more important to him was the knowledge that he was rapidly amassing enough prize money to buy his freedom. Another season as successful as this one and he would be a freedman once more, able to stand with pride by his lover's side.

Publius arrived at the school one evening in unusually high spirits. His centurion had given him the news he had been awaiting for so long: he had been appointed to the Praetorian Guards, the Emperor's own bodyguard, and would shortly be leaving for Rome. This must have been what Fortuna meant when she had predicted his glorious future. Paris turned cold at the news. He tried to be pleased for the soldier, knowing that the promotion was the fulfilment of a long-held ambition. But he could not hide his sense of fear and loss.

Publius, who had learned to read Paris' feelings no matter how carefully he tried to conceal them, reassured the gladiator that he would be faithful to him forever. The Praetorians were given generous leave and they would spend every moment together. But Paris, who had been used to seeing his lover every day, felt a void opening up in his life. He suddenly realised how much he had come to depend on the man. Facing the most fearsome opponent in the ring was nothing to him, but the idea of losing Publius filled him with terror.

Some days later, Corax summoned Paris to his chambers. 'It wasn't just the public you impressed at the Apollo games. Scouts from the Roman gladiator schools were present. They are constantly on the lookout for new attractions for the great games staged under the auspices of the Emperor in the arenas of Rome.'

Paris' heart began to race and he flushed pink.

Corax mistook the young man's expression for one of concern. He hurried on: 'As you know, there are no lanistas like myself in Rome, just procurators recruiting for the great Roman gladiator schools on behalf of the Emperor. The Ludus Magnus, the principal school of the Empire, requires your services.' The lanista looked uneasy. 'I'll admit they made a very generous offer. But the fact is that one does not refuse an order from the Emperor himself. Of course you will be exposed to much greater danger in the Roman arena where all gladiatorial combats are to the death. You are to report for training two weeks from today.'

Paris could no longer contain his delight. He and Publius were to be together again – and in Rome! 'I must tell Publius the news,' he cried, beaming broadly and running from the room. Praise to the goddess Fortuna, thought Paris as he raced down the stairs to the palaestra where he knew his lover was waiting.

The port of Ostia was the hub of the Empire's vast network of trade routes. Long before Paris sighted the harbour itself, its presence was signalled by the heavy traffic of ships large and small. The gladiator stood rooted to the deck, fascinated by every detail of the voyage. In all directions, the blue-green waters teemed with ships and boats of every description, from the four corners of the earth, all heading for Rome.

The characteristic square Roman sails hung limp in the humid air of early August. Sailors heaved on clumsy oars in order to carry their vessels the last few miles of their journey.

Paris was spellbound, however, by the fleets of long-distance triremes and quinquiremes. Some were merchant vessels and others military craft, festooned with fluttering flags and standards. Banks upon banks of oars, dipped and rose from the water with perfect precision, trailing rainbows behind them. In the flat calm of high summer, the sleek ships sped across the glassy surface, their course straight as a javelin's flight. A trireme, Paris had heard, could make the voyage from Rome to Alexandria in only three days. The thought took his breath away.

There was some delay in entering the harbour due to the numbers of craft coming and going. Publius had preceded him to the capital by a week, and Paris could not wait to rejoin his lover. When Paris' boat finally docked at one of the busy quays, he was delighted to see Publius waiting for him, looking splendid in his new uniform: crimson plumes and tunic, helmet and armour of silver and gold.

Although Paris was escorted by two guards from the school in Pompeii, he was no longer treated as a prisoner. He was accorded the trust that a master would place in his most powerful slaves - a steward or a tutor. After all, he was a champion of the arena with a glittering career ahead of him. Besides, his determination to win his freedom was well-known.

Publius' uniform drew awed whispers and glances, as they walked through the teeming harbour: everyone recognised a Praetorian. He stared sternly ahead, pretending not notice, but every now and then shot a mischievous smile at Paris, delighted that the young man could see for himself how important his lover had become.

When they arrived at the jetty where the ferries left for Rome, a decrepit old boatman almost fell at Publius' feet: 'Your worship, I beg you: do me the honour of travelling in my humble bark.' Publius obliged and immediately the crowds on the jetty scrambled after him, until the boatman had to fight them off with an oar in case they sank the battered old vessel, which, if anything, was in worse condition than its owner. Groups of girls sat staring at Publius throughout the journey, exchanging observations behind their hands.

As they rowed up river, it seemed that the rows of warehouses would never come to an end. Streams of slaves unloaded boxes, bales, crates, sacks, chests and coffers which were hauled, carried or winched into the vast storehouses. This is the might of Rome, Paris marvelled - such boundless riches pouring daily into the capital from all over the world.

Huge aqueducts striding purposefully across the countryside, were the first sign that they were drawing close to the city. But nothing could have prepared the young gladiator for his first sight of the capital. Suddenly they rounded a bend and Paris knew that they were in Rome.

A panorama of soaring palaces, temples, theatres and circuses glowed in the golden sunlight of evening, their gilded roofs ablaze. It was a sight more splendid than any of the attempts to portray it in frescos which Paris had seen in great villas. Yet somehow it was like a painting - unreal in its perfection and glory. The Emperor Augustus had claimed that he had found a city of brick and left a city of marble. The Emperors who had succeeded him had continued his programme of building and the whole city appeared to be freshly minted. Indeed new buildings were under construction on all sides.

Publius excitedly pointed out various landmarks, eager to show off his knowledge of the capital to his lover - the palaces of the Palatine Hill, the Temple of Jupiter on the Capitol, the Theatre of Marcellus. They even glimpsed the new Flavian amphitheatre, an edifice greater than any that had gone before it – even in Rome.   Paris heart beat faster as Publius identified this magnificent structure with its soaring tiers of arches. Corax had told him that, as a gladiator of the Great School, he would certainly fight there once it was completed.

As they drew alongside the city streets and caught glimpses of squares between pillared buildings, Paris was almost surprised to see that it was actually inhabited. People lived and worked here just like in any other city. What kind of people must they be, he wondered?

'Couldn't take money from you, your worship,' said the boatman touching his brow obsequiously as they disembarked. Publius winked at Paris, giving the man not only the fare but also a generous tip. The boatman's gesture had been carefully calculated: he knew it would not do for a Praetorian to be seen as a cheapskate.

They hired a litter to take them to the Ludus Magnus, where Paris would live and train. The guards followed on foot. As they passed the Palatine Hill, Publius pointed out his barracks - they were a short walk from the school. Everything would be just as it had been before thought Paris: no - it would be even better.

Having delivered Paris safely to his destination, the guards from Pompeii took their leave. The guards of the Ludus Magnus escorted Paris to the study of Cotilus, the procurator of the school. Publius accompanied his lover and the guards were too much in awe to question his presence.

'Who's this then?' demanded Cotilus when Publius followed Paris into his study.

'A friend I knew from Pompeii.'

'Friends in high places,' muttered the procurator, trying to sound unimpressed, as he ferreted through a pile of scrolls on his desk.

'I was stationed there with the Urban Cohorts, sir,' Publius explained. Cotilus looked up sharply, thinking that Publius was mocking him with his polite tone. But the soldier's expression was sincere.

The procurator pulled open a scroll and peered at it short-sightedly. 'It says here that your name in the ring is Apollo. Well that won't do here,' he grumbled. 'It would be seen as blasphemy.' He glared at Paris for a moment with some distaste. Then his eyes lit up. 'With that mane of hair, why don't we call you the Lion. That has the right ring to it for a hero - proud yet lethal.'

Paris turned to Publius who nodded his approval.

The procurator rubbed his hands together looking very pleased with himself. He peered at the scroll again. 'You're a myrmillo. Let's take a look at your armour and weapons.'

The guards had left Paris' small bundle of possessions beside him and it did not take long to fish out his equipment.

'You'll need a new suit of armour,' Cotilus rasped. 'That rubbish may be fine for the provinces but not in the arenas of Rome.'

Paris looked crestfallen: he had always thought his armour rather fine. Corax had let him take it as a parting gift.

'If your name is to be the Lion, then your armour should be golden. I'll have you measured for it tomorrow. I hope my investment turns out to be worth it,' said Cotilus, observing Paris through narrowed eyes. 'Corax said you were always very willing. And of course your record is impressive.

We've assigned you quarters suitable for the finest gladiators. I think you will find them satisfactory. Report for drill tomorrow at the first hour. You may go.'

'I have a request,' said Paris

'Yes?' snapped the procurator.

'I would like to keep my private life completely separate from my work in the ring,' said Paris. 'I would like to wear my helmet at all times in the arena and be known to the public simply as the Lion.'

Publius shot him an anxious look.

The procurator said nothing, his eyes flicking backwards and forwards from Paris to Publius. A look of cunning crossed his features. 'I see. We wouldn't want to besmirch the honour of the Praetorian Guards by having them associated with the Ludus Magnus of Rome, now would we? Well, I will ensure that no one outside the school will know your real name. The men here pride themselves on their strict code of loyalty: your fellow gladiators will not betray your secret. But it will be up to you to make sure that you maintain your cover by wearing your helmet at all times in public.'

Before they left, Publius asked for permission to take Paris to his barracks that night and indeed if he might escort him around the city whenever they were both off-duty. 'I suppose if he's in the custody of a Praetorian, I can ask no more,' Cotilus retorted with a quizzical look at Publius. 'As long as he reports for training on time and fighting fit, you have my permission.'

It was dark when they ventured out into the streets of the city again. The place was transformed. There was no moon and the narrow alleys were now completely deserted. 'Rome is a dangerous place at night,' Publius warned – 'full of pickpockets and murderers. Law-abiding citizens stay at home and bar their doors. But don't worry, no one will touch a Praetorian.'

It was certainly reassuring to have Publius by his side as they threaded their way through a maze of dark streets. Publius knew of an inn which served good food and provided private rooms where they could talk undisturbed. Despite the fact that it was pitch-dark, hawkers had spread their wares over the narrow pavements and it was almost impossible to take a step without tripping over a terracotta bread oven or a pot of stew. Voices came out of the blackness, offering goods of every kind. Some simply offered themselves. Delivery carts, banned from the city by day, rumbled in a continuous stream along the city streets, like a shadowy funeral cortege. Paris clung to Publius' cloak, scared that they might be separated. If they were, he was sure he would never be found again – alive, at least.

It was a relief to be received into the light and safety of the inn. Although it was only days since they had last seen one another, the two men had much to talk about – Paris excitedly described his journey by sea while Publius spoke enthusiastically about his new posting.

Although the Praetorians were meant to be the Emperor's own bodyguard, in reality there were traitors among them, bribed by those who wished to destroy the Emperor Titus. In his first days on sentry duty at the palace, Publius himself had helped to defeat an assassination attempt against the ruler by rebel Praetorians. It was said that Titus' own brother, Domitian, who wished to claim the office for himself, was behind the conspiracy.

Publius' part in the affair had brought him to the Emperor's attention. His eyes shone as he spoke of the man. 'He is loved by all who know him and is a friend to everyone, without any airs and graces. He even calls us soldiers by name. And his only wish is for the good of his people. That is all he ever talks about in public and in private.'

Publius showed Paris a finely wrought gold and silver medal which he had received from the Emperor's own hands as a reward for saving his life. At Titus' special request, Publius, together with several others who had proved their loyalty, was now permanently assigned to the palace as a member of an elite corps of personal bodyguards.

After supper, Publius asked the gladiator if he would like to visit some of the famous places of the city. But no sooner had he spoken than both men burst out laughing. They wanted one thing only and, hiring a torchbearer to light their way, hurried to Publius' quarters at the barracks.

It was a week since they had slept in each other's arms, but it seemed years. They made love as though it were the first time and fell into a peaceful sleep, their limbs locked together. Just before the first hour of the day, Publius dropped Paris at the school with a promise that they would meet that evening.

Although he was aware that he still had a lot to learn, Paris' first days at the great gladiator school of Rome came as a shock. Given the vast spaces of the capital's amphitheatres, the style of fighting was different to that which Paris had been accustomed in the small arenas of Campania.

Professional gladiators were expected to use the vast expanses of the Roman rings, indulging in long chases and complicated manoeuvres, zig-zagging and doubling back, in order to baffle their assailants. As a myrmillo, Paris would generally be pitted against the retiarius, with his net and trident. Running was one of the main techniques employed by the netman, who would flee from his adversary only to whirl round abruptly and snare the other gladiator in his net.

Once he had realised what was required, Paris rose to the challenge of the new approach. Publius, who continued to drop by whenever he could to keep an eye on the young gladiator's training, noticed a rapid improvement in his skills. Indeed, this style of fighting made full use of Paris' strong points - speed and agility.

Training at the Ludus Magnus took place in a miniature amphitheatre, a fraction of the size of a full-scale arena. Cotilus was constantly present, wringing his hands and urging the men to remember that their moves would have to be much bolder in a real performance. The inauguration of the Flavian amphitheatre, which had been begun by the Emperor's father, the divine Vespasian, would be the highlight of next year's season. The vast marble edifice, situated right next to the Ludus, was nearing completion. Its huge marble pillars and arches could be seen clearly from the palaestra, overshadowing the school. Much of the amphitheatre was still obscured by scaffolding. It was constantly crawling with slaves and the chipping of chisels and ringing of hammers kept up a deafening chorus. At night, building continued by torch-light.

Cotilus was aware that all eyes would be on the gladiators of the Ludus Magnus, the first school of the Empire. They would be expected to put on a terrific show in the finest arena the world had ever seen. The furious building activity put him in a continuous state of nerves. 'The Ludus Magnus of Rome, and this shower is the best we can do,' he would moan as he watched the men exercise: 'You scum will be the ruin of me - mark my words.'

In the school of Pompeii, Paris had fought with the most common types of gladiator – Thracians, secutors, myrmillos and retiarius'. Here, warriors from all over the Empire met in combat according to their local customs: Norsemen with long blond plaits who fought with javelins, Britons who painted themselves blue, Greek Hoplomachi in full armour and armed with pikes, and Essedarii in chariots.

A number of the most famous gladiators had already earned fortunes, and even their freedom. They continued to fight, because they enjoyed the glory, the money and the sexual favours that success in the arena attracted. Paris was immediately befriended by two such men – Pugnax and Iaculator, both secutors, who constantly invited him to riotous parties at their villas or on drinking binges around the city's most infamous taverns. The young gladiator would politely refuse. He and Publius spent all of their spare time together. In his first few weeks, Paris was still spellbound by the city and there were so many monuments to visit, splendid works of art to enjoy and, above all – the theatre.

One afternoon, Publius borrowed a chariot from the barracks and the two young men set out for the great shrine of Fortuna at Praeneste. The oracle confirmed the message they had received from the goddess at her temple in Pompeii: glory for both men. But this time she was more specific: for Paris, the glory of the people and for Publius, the glory of the Empire. That was as it should be, said the two men as they journeyed back to Rome: Paris was a gladiator while Publius was a soldier.

Towards the end of August, Publius arrived earlier than usual at the school one morning. His expression was grim. He and Paris had not seen each other for a day and a night, as the Guard had been on sentry duty at the palace. 'The city has not slept,' he told Paris. 'Even now the streets are empty: the entire populace is gathered on the Capitol and the Janiculum Hill. Titus himself watched all night from the Palatine.'

'But what has happened?' Paris demanded of his lover, who, in his agitation had failed to explain himself clearly.

'Yesterday, black clouds were visible far to the south. They grew in size until night fell when they became clouds of fire. By evening the news had reached the city: Vesuvius has erupted. It seems that Campania has been laid waste.'

'Hopefully it will not be as bad as the earthquake that killed my parents during Nero's reign.'

'Far worse, it seems. Those who managed to escape say that Pompeii has been swallowed up with thousands of its citizens. Stabiae, too. The destruction may have reached as far as Misenum.'

Paris gave a low whistle of astonishment.

'Many of those who have reached the capital have been driven half mad with fear, gibbering that the world is at an end.'

'What can such destruction signify? It is a terrible omen.'

'The Emperor wept as he watched the clouds of fire and as fresh reports arrived. He has already despatched entire cohorts of legionaries to the region to set up camps for those who have lost their homes and to dig out survivors.'

'Such a terrible calamity cannot bode well for his reign.'

'No one dared mention the subject in the palace. There are even rumours going round the city, started by the Jews, that this tragedy is the retribution of the Hebrew God for Titus' destruction of their city.'

'What of our friends?' Paris wondered aloud. He thought of Corax and the gladiators who had shown him kindness. And then there was Bion. Had the villa of Diogenes survived? And Lucius? he thought, in spite of himself.

'It may be weeks or even months before we will know,' replied Publius.

In the wake of this disaster, the plans for the inaugural games of the new amphitheatre took on a new importance. To make matters worse, plague was sweeping the city - it was said that, at its height, 10,000 men and women were succumbing to the disease every day. Most evenings, Paris and Publius dined at the school or at the barracks of the Praetorian guards, preferring to avoid public places. When walking the streets, they would choose a longer, quieter route to avoid the crowds around the Forum. Some parts of the city, worst hit by the plague, were best avoided altogether.

When hurrying back home at night along the quiet streets on the outskirts of the capital, the ghostly shapes of carts loaded with shrouded bodies would pass them by. The two men would shrink against the wall, pulling their cloaks over their heads to protect themselves from contamination and in order to shield their eyes from sights which could bode no good for any man. By night, towering funeral pyres beyond the city walls, belching fire and smoke, could be seen from the Palatine. Paris and Publius watched them in silence.

One night early in the new year, the most terrible disaster of all struck the city. A fire broke out in the Flaminia district, spread to the Capitol, and destroyed the Temple of the Capitoline Jupiter, the principal temple of Rome. By the light of the flames, crowds could be seen gradually filling the Forum and the surrounding squares, silent, eyes fixed on the burning building.

With blind faith, the people looked to the Emperor to reverse the tide of calamity. If the first city of the Empire could be buffeted in this way by the gods, perhaps the world was indeed at an end.

When Titus announced 100 days of games in the new Flavian amphitheatre, therefore, the reaction of the populace was ecstatic.

Posters announcing gladiatorial combats began to appear everywhere - on the walls of houses and shops, even on tombstones. 3,000 pairs of gladiators would fight and 5,000 wild beasts specially imported by the Emperor from all over the world would be slaughtered in a suitably spectacular inauguration of this wonder of art and science.

Publius and Paris would exchange secret smiles as they eavesdropped on crowds eagerly discussing a freshly painted notice. Who was this new gladiator who called himself the Lion? people asked one another. Was he worth a gamble?

Rome – and the world - had never seen anything to equal the new amphitheatre. In addition to almost eighty entrances for the public, one, the Gate of Life, had been reserved for gladiators to enter directly into the arena for the opening parade. On the first day of the games, once the entire crowd was seated and the Emperor had arrived through his own private gate, the gladiators of the Ludus Magnus, who had been brought from the school in carts, appeared in formation to a blaze of trumpets and the strains of a fifty-piece orchestra. The crowd went wild, showering the fighters with flowers, ivory tickets and papyrus programmes.

As Paris looked up through the eye-holes of his helmet, it seemed that the entire population of the capital had been packed into the tiers of the arena which towered heavenwards on all sides. The faces at the top - slaves and women - were mere pinpricks.

The attention of the crowd was immediately drawn to the new young gladiator. Unlike his colleagues, who were dressed in purple and gold tunics and whose armour and helmets were carried behind them by slaves, Paris was already helmeted and fully equipped for combat. He was immediately identifiable as the Lion.

Shrewdly, like the showman he was, Cotilus had ordered one of the finest suits of armour ever seen in Rome for his young protege. Shoulder, arm and leg guards; belt, scabbard and sword hilt, were covered in the finest gold. It was the helmet, however, that was most striking. Cotilus had asked for it to be sculpted in the form of a lion's head, surmounted by a leaping dolphin, as the fish was the myrmillo's symbol. Long vertical slots had been cut into the back of the helmet, narrow enough not to admit the point of a sword or a trident but wide enough to allow Paris' hair to be pulled through in a spreading golden mane.

The posters had proclaimed that the Lion would fight on the third day of the festival. That afternoon, the amphitheatre was packed to bursting. Though a hundred thousand spectators could be packed into the building and the tickets were free, on this occasion the demand was so great that they changed hands at record prices. The superstitious Romans, attracted by Paris' dazzling costume and the mystery surrounding his identity, had bet record amounts on his success in the match.

The gleaming bronze gates swung smoothly open and Paris saw the vast expanse of sand stretch before him. A purple awning covered the ellipse of the arena so that only a small circle of sky could be seen. The canopy protected the audience from the harsh rays of the afternoon sun, but it also meant that the air was stifling. Though a fresh layer of sand had been laid since the wild beast hunts of the morning and the whole area doused with perfume, the stench of blood was overpowering in the heat.

The multitude sent up a resounding cry as they caught sight of Paris. But his attention was focused on a single figure - the retiarius.

Tall and powerfully built, the other gladiator prowled towards him from the other side of the ring, trident and net in either hand, poised to be thrown. Suddenly they were both sprinting across the arena at top speed. Paris, his eyes never leaving the other man for a second, was able to second-guess his feints and crafty manoeuvres.

The crowd went wild with excitement at the speed of the action. Thousands of heads turned in unison as the men dodged each other, flashing from one side of the arena to the other.

A chant of 'Lion' started high up on the stands. It rolled rapidly down to the front seats like a flash flood, swelling to a roar that rocked the building. Then Paris pulled a masterstroke. He turned his back on the retiarius and pretended to acknowledge the cheers of the crowd. The netman, who had been following a path parallel to that of Paris, seeing his chance, hurtled directly towards him. The chant stopped abruptly. A groan went up from the crowd. They shot to their feet as one man, shouting instructions. From the corner of his eye Paris could see Cotilus desperately signalling and calling to him to turn, though his cries were drowned in the general hullabaloo.

The retiarius cast his net and still the Lion did not turn. Cotilus at the side of the ring made a gesture of despair. Timing his move to the split second, Paris sprang to one side. He had judged the trajectory of the net from the sound of the weights whistling towards him and avoided it by a hair's breadth.

Paris spun round to face his opponent. Panicked, the other man threw his trident. Paris neatly side-stepped this as well. The retiarius stood rooted to the spot. He was now completely defenceless. He turned desperately for advice from his lanista who was bawling at the top of his voice from the other side of the arena, though not a word could be heard above the din.

Before the retiarius had time to gather his wits, Paris was upon him and had pinned him the ground. 'He's had it,' went up the traditional cry from the crowd. By now the stands were in chaos as those rooting for the Lion rushed to collect their winnings. Waves of movement swept across the tiers, like the agitated leaves of plane trees, as thumbs wagged excitedly. The chilling chant which spelt death for the loser began to thunder round the marbled splendour of the amphitheatre: 'Cut his throat!'

Holding his sword against the retiarius' neck, Paris looked calmly in the direction of the Emperor's box. When he was present, he was editor of the games and his was the last word. Titus was known and loved by the people for agreeing to their wishes. His decision was certain. A cry of approval went up when a white handkerchief fluttered down from the Imperial box. Suddenly the arena was silent but for a low mutter like wind through a pine forest.

Paris looked down, impassively, at the retiarius. The man's beauty struck him, vaguely, for the first time. His opponent, eyes blank with defeat, stared back at the immobile golden mask of the helmet. The vanquished gladiator wore an expression between puzzlement and pleading, as he lay stretched out on the sand. Paris noticed the imperceptible trembling of his sleek muscular body as he waited, rigid, for the death-blow. Paris raised his sword and then plunged it downwards in an elegant arc. A murmur of appreciation ran through the crowd, quickly followed by an exultant cheer as a fountain of blood rose and fell.

Striding from the arena, Paris thought he could hear the shrill screams of women, slicing through the general shout of approval, crying out not in fear or horror, but in lust. Or was it his own blood ringing in his ears?

The assembled host exploded into applause once again as the golden Lion emerged from the depths of the amphitheatre into the Emperor's box. Paris could not help glancing towards Publius who was standing on guard behind the throne, looking magnificent in his crimson uniform.

Titus sprang to his feet and hurried down the steps towards Paris. He had a handsome face and a powerful body, thought Paris: he did not look forty. 'So, young Lion, you have the whole of Rome agog as to your true identity. Are you the son of a nobleman as they say?' He placed a firm hand on Paris shoulder and leaned close to him. 'Surely your Emperor might know your secret?' he added in an undertone.

Seeing Titus at close quarters for the first time, Paris could understand why Publius was so fond of him. The young gladiator could see that Emperor's interest and smile were genuine.

'How could I refuse Caesar?' Paris stammered. 'I would just ask one favour.' Paris saw Publius shift slightly at this.

'And how could I refuse one who has adorned my father's amphitheatre with such a glorious victory.'

Ben Elliott

'My request is simple, Caesar. I would prefer to reveal myself to you alone.'

'Of course,' Cried Titus, laughing at the young man's earnestness. Taking him by the arm the Emperor led Paris into the shade of a beautifully decorated chamber, hidden from the eyes of the spectators by a curtain of imperial purple. An excited buzz ran round the tiers as the two small figures disappeared. It was unheard of for the Emperor to take such an interest in a gladiator.

'So let's have a look at you,' said Titus, heartily.

Paris was already extricating himself from the helmet. It took longer than usual, because it was fitted so closely to his head and the locks were more complicated than on most helmets. Besides, he had to draw his hair carefully through the slots or tufts of it would be pulled out.

'Well,' said Titus, moving round the gladiator, to observe him from all sides. 'You may not be the son of a nobleman – or at least I do not recognise you – but nor is the story true that your looks were disfigured by fire in the eruption of Vesuvius. I wonder how that one started? But why hide such a handsome face?'

Paris gave a sheepish smile and shrugged.

'Don't worry, I'll let you keep your little secret. Now I have seen your face, I'm sure it is an honourable one.'

Once Paris had replaced his helmet, Titus led him by the arm back onto the balcony. 'As you know I favour Thracians myself. It's my brother Domitian who roots for the myrmillos. But you, young man, have almost made a convert of me.'

The crowd were delighted at the special attention given by the Emperor to their favourite. 'Can you believe it: a myrmillo as brave as a Thracian?' Titus called to the spectators as he handed the prize money to Paris. The crowd roared with laughter. 'We'll show those Thracians,' a rough voice called back from the crowd. The Emperor continued this banter as Paris did a lap of honour around the arena, holding his prize aloft: a silver plate was piled high with gold coins, each bearing the head of the Emperor and, on the reverse, a tiny picture of the new amphitheatre.

Having removed his helmet and armour in a dressing room under the arena, Paris slipped out of one of the public exits and threaded his way through the excited throng towards the gladiator school.

'He kills so beautifully, this young Lion,' murmured a woman's voice. Paris turned to see two Vestal Virgins in their distinctive white robes.

'Imagine how he must wield his sword in the bedchamber,' replied the other Vestal. With bell-like laughter, the two women strolled off arm in arm towards their temple.

Paris smiled to himself. The Emperor was right: he was the talk of Rome.

CHAPTER 8

In the hundred days of games decreed by the Emperor, Paris was billed three times. His third fight earned him his third victory in the Roman arena. Already he had enough money to purchase his freedom, he thought with satisfaction, as he stripped off his armour in a private dressing room under the arena after the fight. Since he was the main attraction, he had been last on the programme that day. Publius would soon be off duty and the young gladiator, now dressed as a simple citizen, had arranged to meet him in the new baths Titus had built right next to his amphitheatre. Paris checked each piece of equipment carefully before leaving a slave to pack it away and return it to the school.

The vaulted passageway outside his dressing room always reminded Paris of a busy street or covered market, constantly bustling with the huge numbers of workers required behind the scenes. There were several of these thoroughfares on the lowest of three levels under the arena. The public, who watched scenery, thousands of wild beasts and fighters appear from nowhere and vanish again at the end of the performance, had no idea that it was all made possible by the existence of a city beneath their feet.

Before a show, the noise in this labyrinth was deafening - the howling of wild beasts, the screams of condemned criminals, the shouts of stagehands raising scenery and cages through trapdoors. Now that the games were over, the atmosphere was comparatively calm as painted flats and empty cages were stored away. Only distant cries of wounded gladiators and bestiarii could be heard as surgeons tended them in the subterranean infirmary.

A stench of blood from hundreds of carcasses, animal and human, pervaded the maze of passages. Despite the efforts of an army of cleaners whose job it was to swill down the floors and brush the gore into waste channels, the smell was indelible.

Even on the hottest days, Paris felt the chill of the tomb in this underground metropolis. Though killing was his trade, he feared the shades of the departed and it seemed to him that they lingered in their thousands in this place of death, lost on their way to the underworld. The gladiator wove his way rapidly along the dimly lit stone corridors and up narrow stairways towards the light and warmth of the outside world. Turning sharply at the top of a steep staircase, Paris collided head-on with a young slave. 'Watch where you're going, lad,' he chided briskly.

'Paris?'

The gladiator squinted in the gloom. He felt the hairs stirring on his arms and shrank against the dank stone wall, instinctively making a sign with his hands to ward off evil spirits. 'Bion?' he whispered.

The slave leaped upon Paris, flinging his arms around his neck and kissing his face like a puppy in the arms of its master. It was obvious that he was no ghost.

'You're alive,' murmured Paris when he managed to disentangle himself for a second.

'You too,' exclaimed Bion. 'I had no news of you after the disaster in Pompeii and feared the worst. Many of the gladiators were lost - Corax, too.'

'Corax?' gasped Paris remembering the fair treatment he had received in the school of the veteran lanista.

'And Lucius?' asked Paris, after a pause.

'Dead,' replied Bion quietly. 'Diogenes was strangely upset at first. But he soon got over it.'

To Paris' surprise, he felt grief for his former lover welling up inside him. He fought back the tears: determined not to mourn for the man who had condemned him to remain a slave.

Although he tried to sound nonchalant, he could see that Bion caught the break in his voice as he asked: 'And the villa?'

'Completely destroyed along with the entire estate.'

'So how did you escape?'

'A miracle - or so Diogenes believes. He consulted the augurers at the temple of Isis in Pompeii shortly before the July elections. The goddess predicted victory, but added that he should return as soon as possible to Alexandria in order to avoid disaster. Well, as you probably heard, she was right about the first part: Diogenes was elected duumvir, the office he has always craved. As far as the warning was concerned, he was convinced that the crops were about to fail or that one of his Egyptian stewards was cheating him. So immediately after the elections we set sail with the fleet for Alexandria.

'Diogenes was puzzled to find that his affairs there were all in order - business was booming, in fact, so he stayed on longer to meet with merchants from the East to discover new goods he could import to Rome. In the meantime, I enjoyed myself visiting the inns and taverns of the city, learning all the latest songs. Remind me to sing some to you later.'

'Of course,' laughed Paris,' but go on with your story.'

'Diogenes decided to make the return journey by way of Numidia to open new trade routes for the import of wild beasts. By then, it was the beginning of September - almost the end of the sailing season - and so we made haste for Pompeii, before the storms began. We made few stops and no news reached us on the journey.

'The first sign that something was wrong was when we spotted Mount Vesuvius on the horizon. But was it? It was in the right place, but it was the wrong shape. At first, we thought we had been driven off course. Then we reached land and found that the port was gone and where the city had been was a black, smoking plain. We headed for Puteoli and there we heard the full story of the disaster.'

'So the augurers of Isis were right,' breathed Paris.

'Yes, and since then Diogenes has offered sacrifice at her temple twice a day in thanksgiving for his narrow escape.'

'Is he here?' asked Paris, glancing around in alarm: it would be safer for his former master to believe him dead.

'Yes,' replied Bion. 'When we realised that the villa had been destroyed, Diogenes was not too concerned. For him, the worst of it was that he was now duumvir of a non-existent city. All the money spent on games, the currying favour with rich and powerful citizens had gone to waste. So he decided to concentrate his efforts on Rome instead. He is planning to sponsor games here in this amphitheatre. Already he has a contract to import sand and wild beasts.'

'Bion, my friend,' smiled Paris, taking his hand. 'The gods be praised for this happy turn of fate. I was sure that you had perished.'

'And I believed the same of you. I hear there are families who were split up in the confusion who are still being reunited almost a year later. But I've been talking so much, you still haven't told me why you are here.'

'Bion, you are one of my few true friends. I will tell you my story since we last met, but first I must swear you to secrecy.'

The slave gave his word, gasping in astonishment when Paris revealed that he was the mysterious gladiator known as the Lion. As they talked, Paris realised how unhappy Bion had become in his master's service following his own departure and Diogenes' break with Lucius.

'You once told me, my friend, that you would always be a slave.'

Bion nodded, his features taking on a serious expression.

'How would you feel if I were to ask you to be a slave in my household?'

The slave's eyes shone.

'I can certainly afford it. In fact I have all sorts of plans for the future and you could play an important part in them. Of course we would not really be master and slave, but friends as we have always been.'

Bion hugged Paris excitedly: 'And I could dance at your parties and sing the latest songs. Would you like to hear one now?'

'Later, my friend. Later.'

Paris was out of breath when he arrived at the baths. It was a warm summer evening and it seemed that the entire male population of the city had turned out to sample the Emperor's magnificent new building. The palatial halls and chambers teemed with naked bodies of every shape and colour.

When Paris spotted his lover, he paused for a moment. The sight of the tall, lean figure, with its long hard muscles, still had a powerful effect on the gladiator. A slave was scraping Publius with a strigil. The soldier gracefully moved his body this way and that to accommodate the smooth strokes of the instrument. Even after all these months, Paris felt his balls tighten and his manhood stir at the sight. He blushed, glancing round to see if other bathers had noticed. An erection or even a large member was an object of interest in the baths and always attracted an audience.

Paris hired an attendant and joined his lover. Excitedly, he told of his encounter with Bion and Publius shared his joy in the reunion.

'Now I have to ask you a favour,' said Paris, lowering his voice. 'I have offered to buy Bion from Diogenes. We would be purchasing his freedom, really, though he would continue to work for us as a servant. I doubt if Diogenes remembers you from your sentry duty at the arena in Pompeii, so you would have to carry out the negotiations.'

Publius had one arm raised as the slave scraped a film of oil across the ridges of muscles just under his armpit, that glistened with smooth black hair. He looked up with a frown. 'As you've raised the subject of freedom, what about you? By now you've earned enough to pay for your freedom several times over. Wasn't that the whole point of becoming a gladiator? How can you talk of buying another man's freedom before your own?'

'There'll be time for that,' said Paris a little impatiently. 'And why bother wasting all that cash when sooner or later the crowd - or the Emperor himself - will offer me the wooden sword which guarantees freedom to a gladiator, but at no cost.'

Seeing Publius' look of disappointment, Paris rapidly outlined his plans: 'I'm tired of having to snatch our moments together in surroundings like these. Ever since we met, we've had to rough it in some old barracks or gladiator school. It's time we had a villa of our own. Bion will be our steward, in charge of running the household and all the other servants. You won't find a harder worker – or one more loyal.'

Although he was unhappy with the idea of postponing Paris' freedom and that there was no end in sight to his career in the ring, Publius agreed that the purchase of a villa was a marvellous idea that would allow them to share their lives completely for the first time. The slaves having completed their work with the strigils, the two men moved into one of the magnificent palaestrae, decorated with glowing mosaics.

They were absorbed in an intense discussion on the site and size of their villa and had even descended into the minutiae of styles and colours of furnishings when a large group of young men stopped directly in front of them. The bathers parted to reveal the Emperor, clad only in a towel. He saluted Publius by name and then his eyes slid to Paris. The gladiator detected a spark of humour in them and saw the sides of the Emperor's mouth twitch as he gave the young man a solemn bow. Their eyes locked and Paris saw a flash of understanding, the confirmation of a promise, and, so it seemed to the young gladiator, an imperial blessing. As the party moved off the two lovers looked at each other in astonished silence.

Publius agreed with Paris' suggestion that if the soldier, as a member of the imperial household, was to approach Diogenes, the old merchant would probably accept his bid for Bion. As it turned out, Diogenes agreed to the sale immediately, without even pausing to consult the wishes of the slave, despite the fact that he had been in his household since childhood and had always served him so wholeheartedly. The merchant made no connection between the proud Praetorian and the humble soldier who had patrolled the arena of Pompeii.

After some discussion and searching, the two men decided on a villa on the Caelian hill which overlooked the Flavian amphitheatre, in the shadow of the temple of Claudius. The dwelling was spacious and quiet, shielded from the noise and the heat of the city by a grove of tall slender cypresses. It was conveniently close to the Ludus Magnus and the Palatine, both of which could be seen from its terraces and balconies.

Neither Paris nor Publius had ever owned a house before, so for some weeks they spent much of their spare time choosing furniture and works of art to adorn the rooms. Paris favoured original Greek statuary, which was hard to find and extremely expensive. Publius preferred works on a military theme and was thrilled when Paris bought him an antique bronze chest, carved with scenes of battle, which the salesman claimed had been made for Sulla, the Dictator.

Delighted at his new position as steward of the household, Bion raced from room to room, supervising the shifting of furniture and the hanging of curtains. The cavernous rooms rang with his Alexandrian ditties, which he insisted on teaching to the rest of the servants as he claimed they would work more willingly that way.

When they paused for a meal, he would give impromptu performances of the dances of Gades and the sound of castanets and rhythmic

Ben Elliott

clapping echoed through the marble chambers. Surveying the results of Bion's unorthodox methods, Paris and Publius had to agree that they had worked: the villa had been readied in just a few days and its beauty exceeded their hopes.

'Imagine,' Publius teased his lover on their first night there: 'A gladiator with his own palace right next to the Emperor's. What is the world coming to?'

'A Praetorian guard with his own palace next to the Emperor's,' Paris shot back in a tone of mock surprise. 'What next?'

They were standing on the balcony of their bed-chamber. The hill fell away in a sheer drop below them. By the cold moonlight, over the tops of pines, they could see the Flavian amphitheatre and to the left of it, the Forum and the Palatine.

Paris took his lover's strong hand in his. A cloudbank, shaped like the head of a god, moved across the moon. The trees were bowed by a sudden gust of cold wind. It was now September, a month of storms, and suddenly heavy rain slanted across the scene. The wind lifted the sharp scent of wet pine-needles into the chamber. The amphitheatre blazed ghostly white in a flash of lightning. Gazing out on the storm from the shelter of the balcony, the lovers felt closer than ever.

Publius drew Paris to him. 'This would be perfect,' he whispered, 'if only we could stand together side by side as freedmen. You have the ear of the Emperor and could even be a citizen if you wanted to.'

'I will, I will,' replied Paris softly, smiling at his lover and kissing him gently on the lips. 'Just be patient and we will have everything we want.'

'Don't wait too long,' said his lover seriously. 'You are a great fighter. But the goddess Fortuna has smiled on you. Do not tempt her patience. Remember that you never wanted to be gladiator: the arena is only a means to an end.'

The Ludi Romani, games which had been held in the capital each September for four hundred years, were underway. Paris had two important fights scheduled. Returning to his dressing room under the arena, following his victory in the first bout, he did not notice his lover standing in the shadows at the back of the dark chamber. Paris had been required by the crowd and the Emperor to sacrifice his opponent. He had a way, now instantly recognisable to the crowd, of avoiding the fountain of blood that would shoot up from the victim's neck, so that not a drop would sully his armour. On this occasion, however, when the hot liquid gushed out, to the wild delight of the spectators, he had taken the full force of it on his face and body. He had not consciously intended to do this, but it had given him a strange warm feeling which both thrilled and repelled him.

The metallic reek of fresh blood hit Publius' nostrils the moment the gladiator entered the chamber. He was startled at the sight - as gruesome as an actor's entrance in the last act of a tragedy – and instinctively exclaimed his lover's name. It was only then that Paris became aware of Publius' presence. The gladiator stared at the soldier without recognition or affection. But on his face was a look of exultation that Publius had never seen before.

That night Paris arrived back at the villa very late. Even the servants were asleep, though the faithful Bion was waiting for him, busily chatting to the watchman. Paris was in no mood for Bion's gossip and he cut his friend off in mid-sentence, bidding him goodnight.

As he entered the darkened chamber, Paris could see Publius' long body already stretched out on the bed. Fortunately, he seemed to be asleep, although he was such a quiet sleeper that on more than one occasion, Paris had pressed his ear to the other man's mouth just to make sure he was still breathing.

Without even bothering to remove his sandals, Paris fell back heavily on the bed. He was relieved not to have to face Publius. After their encounter in the dressing room, he felt the need to get away, to be alone.

He did not want anyone poking around in the emotions he experienced in the arena. That part of his life was out-of-bounds. Even he was uneasy looking back on those moments and the strange feelings they aroused. Far back in the mists of time, the games had been instituted in order to appease the spirits of the dead with human sacrifice. Perhaps those shades, with their insatiable lust for blood, took possession of the gladiator in the arena, thought Paris with a shudder. He pushed the thought from his mind.

One thing was certain: although he was in the presence of thousands of screaming spectators, the gladiator was alone in the void of the arena, suspended between death and life. Something happened out there to the professional fighter. Paris was not sure what it was - a kind of elemental force that descended on him - but he did know that it kept him alive. It was something that anyone who had not fought in the ring - not even Publius - could ever understand.

He had needed to be with his fellow gladiators that night. Men like Pugnax and Iaculator. Only they understood. They did not even need to talk about these things, and rough clods that they were, they probably could not have found the words anyway. In the past, Paris had always refused their invitations to drinking bouts and parties. But tonight he had accepted.

They needed to forget too, he thought. That is why they went drinking every night, why they indulged in licentious behaviour and stalked the dark alleyways of the city in gangs, beating and robbing passers-by. Somehow, this conduct was expected of the gladiators; Paris had seen how even the vigiles, who patrolled the streets at night, turned a blind eye to the marauding band of professional fighters.

Drunk and exhausted, he fell into a deep, dreamless sleep.

Paris' evenings took on a new pattern. Most nights he would accompany his colleagues on their binges. Sometimes one of the wealthy gladiators would throw a lavish supper at his villa. The finest wines - usually undiluted - would flow freely. Male and female devotees of the gladiators would also attend and the party would eventually break up as groups and pairs drifted off into quiet corners of the house or garden.

Paris would stagger back to the villa in the small hours. Publius had usually fallen asleep, exhausted from waiting. Sometimes he would open his eyes briefly and throw a wiry arm over Paris' chest. Not once, however, did he question the gladiator on where he had been. In the morning Paris would wake to find Publius had left for the palace. Bion would bring him a herbal brew for his pounding head and he would try, unsuccessfully, to piece together the incidents of the previous night.

At the Plebian Games, the following November, an ecstatic crowd voted Paris the wooden sword of freedom. Publius was on duty in the Imperial box when Titus pressed this honour on the victorious young gladiator. Pandemonium broke out in the stands when Paris turned down the offer and pledged to Emperor and people that he would continue to fight in the arena as a slave. Publius recoiled like a man who has received a blow to the face. But, if the cheers of the people when they voted him the wooden sword had been enthusiastic, now they were ecstatic. The Emperor, too was delighted, clapping the golden gladiator warmly on the shoulder.

That night Paris stayed out late celebrating his triumph with his friends. It was well after midnight when he staggered into the bedchamber at the villa. Publius was still awake, seated with his back to Paris, gazing out over the city. 'Why did you refuse the wooden sword, today?' Publius asked, without turning.

Paris shrugged and sat down heavily on the bed. 'I knew the crowd would like it and they did. Didn't you hear them cheer? There will be other opportunities.'

'You never intend to leave the arena, do you?'

'Why should I?' demanded Paris gruffly, 'when it gives us all this? What have you got to complain about?'

'Do you never wonder how I feel every time I see you fight?' Publius got up from the chair and moved quickly towards the bed. 'Have you forgotten the boon we asked of the goddess so long ago in Pompeii: your freedom? You never wanted to be a gladiator.'

'Well now I do. I am the Lion, the people's favourite.'

'I've watched you change over the past year and it frightens me. I am a soldier. I have killed men: that is my duty. But I never enjoyed it. Do you remember when I was waiting for you in the dressing room during the Ludi Romani? You didn't realise I was there at first. When I looked at you, I saw not the kind and cultured man I fell in love with, but someone with a taste for killing. Not a man. A beast.'

Paris leapt up from the bed. His face was half in shadow. Publius saw a strange, unfamiliar expression flicker across it - whites of eyes flashing and teeth bared in a snarl, like a animal about to attack. With a blinding flash of pain, Publius felt a blow to the side of his neck, blunt and powerful like the swipe of a heavy paw. The next moment, he was sprawled on the cold marble floor.

The gladiator looked down at his lover. Publius stared back with the bewildered look of a beaten dog. Just as when he dealt the coup de grace in the arena, Paris felt nothing. 'Here, I am master,' he growled in a voice Publius did not recognise. Paris turned away and stumbled blindly from the room and down the hill towards the seedy inns of the city where he knew he would find his companions.

It was three days before he returned. His memories were vague after the first night: a blur of low-life taverns and houses of ill-repute. He had not bothered to report to the gladiator school – he feared that Publius might be waiting there for him. Yet as the days passed, his longing for the soldier grew until he could think of nothing else. He waited until everyone was asleep before sneaking into the villa by a side entrance. Not having bathed for days, he knew he must reek of wine and the filth of the streets.

Publius was in the chair by the window. Overcome with fatigue after nights of waiting, he had nodded off to sleep for a moment. The gladiator crossed the room so quietly that Publius was not aware of his presence until he felt his lover's head laid softly in his lap.

The soldier opened his eyes and seeing Paris' golden head, began to stroke it gently.

Paris sighed. 'You know, I have always lived a kind of slavery,' he murmured, without looking up: 'first at my uncle's house and later in Diogenes' household and at the school. But in the arena, I experience a strange power and freedom. It is as though I were possessed by a god – or a demon. And that is what enables me to win. You were right. I have changed over the past months. Fighting, killing has become a need.' He turned his face up to Publius who was listening solemnly. 'It is time for me to give up my life in the amphitheatre. Otherwise, I fear I my lose myself completely – and I may lose you, too.' Paris rested his head on Publius' knee once more. 'I promise that next time I am offered my freedom I will accept. And then I will gladly live as your slave.'

Publius helped Paris to his feet and led him to the baths, where he stripped the gladiator of his filthy clothes and sponged him down. Taking Paris by the hand, the soldier guided him back to their chamber where they clung together, naked on the bed. Paris was so exhausted that he was not sure if he was awake or dreaming: the only thing that seemed real, indeed the only thing that he was aware of, was Publius, the reassuring feel and smell of him.

Publius' mouth was on his, bruising it with urgent kisses, tongue probing wildly. Those kisses: so unmistakable, thought Paris, as he responded with trance-like intensity.

The soldier's long hard body lay along his own shorter, but broad and powerful form. The smooth straight hair on Publius' chest and abdomen ground against the thick blond hair carpeting his own torso. Paris sighed as he felt the weight of his lover's body press down on him. The firmness, the leanness was like that of no other man.

Paris ran his fingertips over the taut, fine-grained skin of Publius' back with its pattern of silken hair. Did any other skin feel that way? he wondered. He was convinced that if he were blind he would recognise Publius by touch alone.

Publius' fingers, moistened with spittle, gently probed the hard button of Paris' anus. The soldier's long arms swung the gladiator's legs back and outwards. Paris flung his head back in a long moan of pleasure as the soldier's sword thrust into that wound which would never heal: no one, no other cock had ever felt like that in Paris' ass.

The two men felt a hunger for each other that was stronger than anything they had experienced before. Almost immediately, Publius began to fuck Paris hard. He dribbled spittle into the gladiator's mouth as Paris held out his tongue to receive it. Their lips locked in a long, hard kiss. A low drone began in the soldier's throat as the driving rhythm of his strokes pushed him towards climax.

Publius' lithe body stiffened, eyes clenched shut. Paris felt the spasms of the soldier's cock against his sphincter as he irrigated the gladiator's guts with a pent-up flood of semen.

As soon as his lover had pulled out of him, Paris greedily wrapped his lips round the other man's still-erect cock, savouring their mingled smells, and slurped like a starving man on the layer of salty semen which coated the firm rod. Only Publius tastes like this, thought Paris, holding the flavour in his mouth like a rare wine.

The taste and smell intensified his burning desire for his lover and Paris longed to deposit his seed in the other man's body as a pledge of their renewed love.

Ben Elliott

Moistening his fingers with the liquid that dribbled from his own ass, Paris lubricated his lover's hole, which was already softening with antici-pation. As Paris carefully introduced his dripping cockhead into the radiat-ing folds of Publius' anus, the soldier strained impatiently against it with the full force of his hips, swallowing Paris' dick in his rectum with a single gulp.

For a moment Paris luxuriated in the feeling of his member sheathed in his lover's flesh. Slowly he began to slide it back and forth. The precise degree of heat in the other man's rectum, its silken lining, the cushion of his large balls as Paris thrust against them: this could only be Publius, he thought.

The soldier and the gladiator struggled fiercely, the one grinding his firm ass, hungry for sperm, the other thrusting obsessively, desperate to plant his seed. As the glow mounted in Paris' loins, and a geyser of sem-inal fluid was unleashed into Publius' body, Paris was overwhelmed by a feeling of recognition.

'No one ever felt the way you do,' murmured Publius as they nestled together afterwards.

Paris smiled. 'Have you been reading my thoughts again?' he enquired, sleepily. He laid his head against Publius' hard chest and wrapped his legs and arms around the other man.

As Paris drifted off to sleep, his eyes, his mouth, his nostrils and his ears were filled with his lover. Publius' touch was imprinted on every inch of his body. Even as he dreamed - stepping from the amphitheatre of Pompeii into his uncle's dining room, through a door into the Ludus Magnus and up a staircase to a strange land he had never seen - Publius was there, always by his side.

The following evening, buffeted by a heavy storm, Paris hurried up the slippery paved road to the villa. Although he had fought his last bout of the season, there had been much to do at the school that day. But he was anxious to return and dine with Publius at the villa, just as they used to do when things were going well between them. Pausing in the shelter of the marble gatepost, he noticed a dark form huddled on the ground at his feet.

The rain ran in blinding rivulets down his brow. Wiping it away with his arm, he stooped and recognised Bion muffled in a cloak. The slave had obviously been waiting for some time as he had fallen into a deep sleep and Paris had to shake him vigorously to wake him.

When he recognised Paris' voice demanding an explanation for his strange behaviour, Bion leapt to his feet and clung to the gladiator's tunic, burying his head in the man's powerful chest. The slave was soaked to the skin. He shook uncontrollably and his teeth were chattering. His dark head bowed, he began to sob like a child.

The rain, hurled against them by strong gusts of wind, stung their legs and faces like needles. Paris took his friend roughly by the arms. 'Look at me, Bion. What's the matter?' he shouted over the howling of the storm.

Still hiding his face, Bion sobbed a few words into Paris' chest, but they were scattered by the wind and rain. All Paris could catch was the single name 'Publius'.

'Publius? What's wrong?' cried Paris, anxiously. 'Is there something the matter? I must go to him.' Bion responded with a mute shake of his dripping curls.

'Why not? Is he here?' Paris pulled away from the slave and headed into the teeth of the gale towards the villa. Surely the differences between them had been resolved. Panic entered his voice: 'Has he gone?'

Bion grabbed Paris' cloak with surprising strength, pulling him back. 'It's too late,' he cried.

As Paris whirled round, Bion looked up at him for the first time, his cloak flapping wildly in the driving rain. Seeing his friend' eyes, swollen from weeping, Paris staggered back against the gatepost. Suddenly he understood.

Publius was dead.

CHAPTER 9

With Publius gone, the villa which Paris had loved so much seemed to die too. In that place which had been the visible expression of their bond, the soldier's absence was palpable. Paris experienced a physical pain, an ache in his chest, when he looked at the chair on the balcony where Publius loved to sit, or the baths where they had passed quiet hours reading poetry to one another, or the shady triclinium where they had spent long evenings dining together.

Now the prediction of Fortuna's oracle at Praeneste was clear. Publius had the glory of the Empire – but in death. He had told Paris of the frequent attempts to murder the Emperor. Domitian, Titus' jealous brother was behind them, he had explained. But why did Publius have to risk his life in order to defend the Emperor? Surely his first loyalty was to his lover, not his ruler? Paris cursed Domitian. He cursed the Emperor. He cursed the goddess. He cursed Publius.

The Emperor decreed a hero's funeral in the Forum for the three Praetorian Guards who had died fighting off the assassins. From the balcony of the chamber that had been theirs, Paris watched the smoke and flames thrown into the night sky by the funeral pyre. He had to force himself even to do this. He could not have endured to witness his lover's flesh sizzling till it fell away in charred lumps.

The urn containing the soldier's ashes was brought to the villa late the same night on the express orders of Titus himself. Paris could not bear to look at it, could not bear to think that all that was left of that smile, that ardour, those long hard limbs, was a puff of grey powder. He hid it away in a chest.

Paris no longer used the bedchamber or the bed which had been specially made for them, choosing to sleep in a small guest bedroom on a narrow couch. In fact he slept very little now. He was constantly turning over in his mind the events leading up to Publius' death, bitterly regretting the lost months when he had preferred the company of his drinking companions to that of his lover. The pain he had caused Publius was unendurable.

If only he had acted differently, Publius might still be here, sleeping silently by his side. What if he had purchased his freedom as soon as he could afford it? Perhaps Publius would have applied for more leave. Maybe, if Paris had not spent so much time away from the villa, his lover would not have volunteered for extra duties.

Bion did all he could to ease Paris' pain. He quietly brought him the dishes he liked best. He read to Paris from his favourite poets. On one occasion he even offered to sing for him. 'Anything but that,' snapped Paris. Instantly regretting the remark, he snatched the slave's hand and squeezed it hard.

Despite Bion's efforts, Paris jumped at any excuse to spend time away from the villa, accepting every invitation offered to him by his gladiator friends. The festival of the Saturnalia in December was a blur of wild debauchery, offering welcome oblivion. Though his revels continued nightly, in the New Year he began to train again at the Ludus. He had asked Cotilus that he should be entered for as many fights as possible when the games began again in April. The arena was the one place where he could truly forget.

The whole of Rome was in agreement: the Lion had never been so fierce as he was that year in the Ludi Megalenses, the games dedicated to the goddess Cybele and the first big event in the annual calendar. He fought like a demon, like one who held life itself in contempt. The rabble crammed the tiers of the Flavian amphitheatre, cheering themselves hoarse, as Paris scored victory upon victory, amassing another fortune in the process. Twice more he rejected the crowd's offer of the wooden sword of freedom.

He had decided to maintain his anonymity. Publius had been the reason he had kept his true identity secret. If he were to reveal it now, his last living link with the soldier would be broken. Besides, the Lion's mystery was an important part of his popularity with the mob. To change that might jinx his success.

'When are you going to throw a party?' Pugnax asked Paris as they lay sprawled around his dining table late one night. 'It's about time, after all the invitations we've given you. And I hear you're rattling about that enormous palace by yourself these days.'

Paris span round, his eyes flashing angrily.

'Well, that's what I heard, anyway,' said Pugnax lamely, holding up a calming hand. 'But you can't trust the gossip in the Ludus Magnus. So, no offence, my friend.'

Maybe the gladiator was right, though. A party would liven the place up a bit and even exorcise the ghosts that haunted him.

When he outlined to Bion the kind of event they would be staging, with hundreds of young male slaves hand-picked for the evening from the finest houses of pleasure in the capital, Paris' chief steward pulled a face. 'I'm no prude, as you know. In fact, it sounds like the kind of party I might enjoy. I just wonder whether this is what Publius would have wanted in the villa.'

'What does that matter?' Paris sighed irritably. 'Right now I need to forget Publius - and I only know two ways to do that: having fun with my friends and competing in the arena.'

Bion shrugged: 'Perhaps a better way to honour his memory would be to buy your freedom and retire. But I'm the last person to give you advice,' he added, hurriedly exiting from the chamber as he spotted Paris' dark expression.

Despite his objections, the arrangements for the party were left to Bion. He did a thorough job, as Paris knew he would, and came up with ideas that the gladiator was sure would surprise and delight his guests.

'You have some beautiful servants,' commented Iaculator to Paris on the night of the party, as they dined in the triclinium that had been specially constructed on the hillside overlooking the amphitheatre. It was a moonlit night, and the city's most famous monuments formed a backdrop to the entertainment of sensual dances and mimes that Bion had prepared.

Paris turned on the gladiator: 'You are not to touch them. A special entertainment has been devised to take place after supper: it will supply more beautiful boys than you could possibly handle in one night, Iaculator.'

'Can't I even have that one?' asked Iaculator indicating Bion, who was watching the dancers from the side of the stage.

'Especially not that one,' replied Paris. 'I don't even consider him a slave: he is a dear friend.'

After supper, the guests were invited to proceed behind the villa to an area hidden from outside eyes by tall cypresses. A wide curtain of pale blue silk was stretched across the garden. It was well lit by tall candelabra, positioned at intervals in front of it, while lamps had been suspended from the trees.

A band, placed to one side, struck up a sinuous melody. Paris smiled to himself as he recognised one of Bion's favourite Alexandrian tunes. At a signal from the steward, stagehands in the trees severed the cords which held up the curtain. As it billowed to the ground, the guests, began to murmur. It took a moment for them to realise exactly what had been revealed. The murmurs turned to cheers. Appreciative looks were directed at Paris as the company burst into applause.

'Gentlemen', proclaimed a hired actor, 'we invite you to storm the Temple of Love.'

At first no one moved, somewhat in awe of the sight before them. Then one or two gingerly approached it and soon the scene resembled a battle staged in the arena as the guests threw themselves into the melee.

Bion's idea had been simple, but inspired. He had built a Temple of naked human bodies lashed into position on a specially constructed wooden frame. All the young men, of a variety of complexions and builds, had been selected for their beauty: each was available for the enjoyment of the guests.

The Temple steps were formed of slaves restrained in crouching positions, offering rows of spread assholes on all four sides of the edifice. Especially tall young men had been secured to the pillars, some with their behinds exposed and some facing outwards like caryatids, all with their arms chained above their heads. Ladders had been conveniently positioned to make the mouths of these young men accessible. The roof was tiled with bodies, alternately facing up or down, while the pediments offered endless permutations of asses, mouths and cocks.

In front of the Temple was an ornate working fountain. For this, Bion had chosen the theme of the love between the warriors Achilles and Patroclus, shown surrounded by their warriors.

Ladders had been provided so that the Temple could be 'stormed'. In other words, the lads could be approached from almost any angle and their orifices and appendages used according to the fancy of the guests. The chains and ropes that held the youths in place were intended more to stimulate the appetites of the gladiators than to prevent escape. The slaves were only too willing to be ravished by the men and were enthusiastic collaborators in Bion's scheme.

The gladiators felt like bees in a rose-garden: there was so much nectar on offer, they could not decide where to suck first. The rows of roses along the temple steps was a major attraction. Not bothering to shed their garments, a group of guests headed straight for the exposed anuses. Lifting up the short skirts of the tunics, they plunged their sturdy cudgels into the boys' ready-greased holes, glistening in the candlelight. The slaves were positioned at a convenient height so that the gladiators were not obliged to stoop.

A chorus of grunts came from all four sides of the Temple as the burly warriors fucked energetically. They had stripped off their tunics to reveal their huge beefy bodies. Beads of sweat shimmered in the hair which covered their torsos and brawny legs. From behind, rows of clenched hairy asses could be seen thrusting to the beat of the band which accompanied the event.

Some of the men devised a game. On certain changes in the music they would pull out in unison from the hole they were screwing, take one step to their left, and lance the next orifice in the row. They found this extremely amusing, guffawing on each change of position.

Meanwhile other gladiators had explored the many delights offered by the Temple. The roof had acquired a second layer as they lay on the carpet of flesh. Some snaked slowly over the roof, allowing soft tongues to explore every part of their naked bodies, while their cocks were devoured by every greedy ass and mouth they encountered.

Men hung from ladders at every height and angle, the better to make use of a pretty mouth or anus. One adventurous fighter clung to the rungs of a ladder so that one of the statues on the pediment of the Temple could tongue his rectum while another sucked on the throbbing gristle of his engorged member.

The band had now ceased and Bion, accompanying himself on a small lyre, was singing his favourite songs to a group of guests pausing for a rest before re-entering the fray. Paris noticed Iaculator among them, smiling and nodding in time to the music.

Half-drunk and flushed with lust, Paris had sampled some of the anuses of the steps, before clambering up to the pillars of the Temple. The blond hair which covered his naked body shimmered in the light of a thousand flames. Half-crouching, the young gladiator's gaze scanned the line of beautiful boys, their arms shackled above their heads like Andromeda by the sea-shore. Paris' long golden hair fanned over his back and his eyes, golden in the firelight, flashed with the untamed spark of a jungle beast's. His arching cock spilt drops of golden pre-cum.

Paris spotted a slender, but well-muscled youth with long dark hair and immediately pounced on the lad. He kissed the young man who responded ardently with a hot, red mouth. Clutching the youth's slender hips, Paris ground his hard tool against the lad's cock, red and rampant. Paris noticed a glimmer of recognition in the young man's eyes as he answered the myrmillo's moves with gyrations of his pelvis. Paris began to pound the lad's cock hard with his own, rubbing the sensitive flesh raw. Their bodies twisted and swayed, locked together like wrestlers in combat. Loose ball-sacs thudded painfully against each other.

The long chains left room to manoeuvre, and Paris swung the lad round, standing back to admire his shapely rear. He gave it a hard slap and watched the red imprint of his hand slowly materialise on the smooth skin. A crack rang out as he whacked the other buttock. The young man thrust his ass towards Paris inviting him to use it. The cheeks parted, revealing a neat line of black hair.

Paris knelt to examine the crack more closely. A tight carmine butthole nestled among the shiny dark curls. Paris teased it with his moistened tongue-tip. It twitched like a sea-anemone. Paris spat on it and it began to open, revealing the velvety darkness inside. Paris was on his feet, roughly manipulating the hole with his fingers. The boy writhed, then let out a long sigh as he felt the full length of Paris' member spear his entrails. His hands clenching the youth's shoulders, Paris fucked him violently. The lad's moans of pleasure were interspersed with sharper cries of pain. But

Paris did not relax his relentless motion.

Although, he was unable to touch himself, the young man's vertical prick pitched and jarred with involuntary spasms. Paris could feel every impulse in the taut grip of the lad's rectum. As he drove his pole ruthlessly into the youth's anal canal, he knew that they were both approaching climax. Tossing back his blond mane, Paris let out a roar and his body jackknifed repeatedly as he released a stream of burning seed into the lad's hungry intestines.

After a split second's delay, the youth heralded his orgasm with a loud yell. His knees shook as his cock reared convulsively, spraying streams of man-juice randomly in all directions. Once their movement was stilled, Paris could feel a tremor shaking the entire sturdy edifice, like a minor earthquake, the combined effect of hundreds of humping men.

Resting his head against the lad's shoulder for a moment, Paris was vaguely aware that something had changed. The grunts and bellows of lovemaking could still be heard but Bion's voice had stopped. Paris felt uneasy. Abruptly, he pulled out of the boy who wheeled round, his lips parted in a look of panic as he saw the long-haired gladiator move away.

Bion and his group of listeners had gone. Paris ran round the Temple searching diligently for a sign of his friend. But Bion was not there. Nor could he see Iaculator or the other guests who had been listening to the songs.

Still naked, Paris raced into the villa, calling Bion's name. The servants, who were busily clearing away after the banquet, had not seen the steward since the guests had retired to the Temple. He rushed out into the garden, heading for the secluded areas at the foot of the Temple of Claudius. Thistles and thorns tore at his skin as he scrambled through the undergrowth, darting first one way then the other.

Struggling painfully through thick brambles, Paris broke into a clearing screened on all sides by an overgrown hedge. He saw a small group of dark naked forms huddled together, silent, watching. A slim figure was silhouetted by moonlight at the end of the clearing, suspended by the arms between two trees: Bion. A burly gladiator, who Paris immediately identified as his drinking partner Iaculator, was fucking the lad hard and seemed to have his hands around the boy's throat. Paris bounded towards the group.

The bystanders scattered in the undergrowth. Iaculator's face, twisted with violence, suddenly went blank as he spotted Paris. He released his grip on Bion's neck and the slave's body hung limp, his head slumped to one side. Iaculator staggered backwards, pulling his rapidly shrinking weapon from the young man's body.

A lattice of bloody streaks and livid bruises covered Bion's back and buttocks. Blood ran down his legs from his rectum.

'Now, Paris, calm down,' appealed Iaculator, slowly backing away. 'He agreed to come.'

'But not to this, Iaculator. He is my oldest friend. I told you to keep your filthy hands off him. Get out of my house. Tell your friends the party's over.'

Bion's neck was badly bruised and, at first, Paris feared he might not survive. But, though he had been severely beaten and half-strangled, he was still alive. His breathing was laboured like that of a child with a high fever. Paris knew that if he had appeared just a few seconds later, it would have been too late.

'Animals, animals,' Paris repeated to himself as he gently sponged his friend's broken body. Worse than animals, he thought: the beasts in the arena had to be forced to fight.

Early the next morning Paris went to Cotilus.

'I wish to buy my freedom,' said Paris. 'I have decided to retire from the arena.'

Cotilus was astonished. He tried everything he could to persuade Paris to at least maintain his commitments for the season. But in the face of the procurator's cajoling, threats and pleas, Paris stood firm. Finally, realising that it was hopeless, and knowing that Paris did, after all, have the right to his freedom, Cotilus gave in.

'I'll be ruined,' he moaned, his head in his hands. 'Such a disgrace for the school. What will the Emperor say?'

Paris smiled. 'I don't think you will have a problem with the Emperor. This is something I should have done a long time ago. You could say it is a debt to a friend.'

'How will the people react? There will be riots in the amphitheatre.'

'Perhaps it's right for the Lion to exit on a note of mystery. And it won't be long before you find another young lad with talent. Just give him an original name and a fine suit of armour. Create a legend around him. You can do it. You did it with me.'

'Paris,' said Cotilus wistfully, shaking his head, 'there will never be another Lion.'

'Keep my secret,' said Paris. 'I don't want to be pestered by admirers. And, you never know, one day, I might be back.'

'If you do ever decide to return, Paris, be sure it's with the Ludus Magnus.'

For the next few weeks, Paris devoted himself to caring for Bion. He paid for the best Greek doctors and priests of Asclepius to tend to the young man's injuries. It was time to leave Rome, this city of violence where he had lost his lover and almost lost his best friend. Paris had been brought up by the sea and he longed for its calming influence. He found a secluded villa right on the coast some miles north of Ostia, where the sea was visible from almost every room. It would be the ideal spot for Bion to recuperate and it would give Paris the peace he craved.

For days, Bion ran a fever and for some time after that he was too weak to talk. Although he had neglected his friend over the past months, Paris suddenly realised how much he missed his company. He even found himself pining for Bion's beloved Alexandrian songs. When it came to organising the move, it became clear to him how much he had relied on his friend to keep his affairs in order. He could not face sorting through Publius' clothes and personal effects, for example, and simply stuffed them randomly into chests.

The sea air speeded Bion's recovery just as Paris had hoped. By June, the slave was able to leave his bed, but Paris would not hear of him doing any work. They would spend their days quietly together, talking over old times in the baths or reading poetry and scenes from plays to one another. Their favourite spot was a dining room with a large bay window looking directly out to sea.

Paris took long walks alone on the sandy shore. Staring out at the becalmed sea, he felt that it reflected the blankness of his existence. After so much success and acclaim, he could see no future ahead. His life seemed to have come to an end.

He had always prided himself on his independence. He needed nobody. Yet he had lost the two men he had loved, Lucius and Publius, and had almost lost his best friend. Now he realised that, in different ways, he had needed all of them.

If he had behaved differently, Paris admitted to himself, he would not be so alone. He regretted bitterly his treatment of Lucius, how he had judged him with the harshness of youth and refused to give him a second chance. Although he thanked the gods for the short time he and Publius had spent together, there was no reason why he and Lucius could not have remained friends. It seemed clear that Lucius had truly loved him and that, after repenting his errors, had been prepared to renounce everything for that love. Paris was able to admit to himself that he had loved Lucius in return and that, though they had been buried under pride and anger, those feelings had remained hidden inside him.

In September, news reached the villa that the Emperor had died - of natural causes. Paris' bitter feelings were reawakened. He was sickened by the irony of it: Publius had died to save a man who would himself be dead in less than a year. Even his heroism had been for nothing: Domitian, Titus' brother and would-be assassin, had succeeded him as Emperor.

One afternoon, as Paris fell silent, halfway through reading one of his best loved poems of Catullus, Bion knelt down beside him placing a hand on his knee.

'We are still alive, you know. And young. It's time to start living again.'

Paris turned to his friend as though emerging from a dream: 'You know, I spent all those months after Publius' death trying to forget. Now I realise that I need to remember. I have an idea, Bion. I would like to build a temple, here by the sea, and dedicate it to Publius and Lucius. After all they were my real family. Apart from you, of course.'

'Let's do it,' said Bion. 'You will never forget them. That is what the temple will show. But then, for their sake, you must start to live again. All the good things you received from them will live on in you.'

Although he knew that sooner or later, he must return to the hurly-burly of daily life, for the time being, Paris enjoyed the peace and seclusion of the villa. The news from Rome filtered through to the villa from servants and acquaintances in the nearby village, usually courtesy of Bion.

Plans for the temple began to occupy all of Paris' time. It would be a simple, round structure in the Greek style and would contain statues of the two men. He had decided to commission a Greek artist to execute the statues, as their work was infinitely superior to that of the Roman sculptors.

There was one problem - the statue of Lucius. When they had moved into the villa in Rome, Paris had commissioned a portrait of himself and Publius: the artist had captured the soldier very well and this would be a great help to the sculptor who was fashioning his statue. In Lucius' case, however, Paris had no access to any likeness. The sculptor would therefore be reliant on their memories and suggestions. And Paris feared that his recollections of Lucius had already grown dim.

The tablet clattered on to the bronze table. 'How can he ask this of me,' Paris demanded angrily. 'I told that money-grubbing old procurator that I was retiring for good and six months later, he's insisting that I return.'

'The Emperor's insisting you return,' corrected Bion, softly.

'According to Cotilus. But then he'd say anything to get what he wants.'

'You know I would be the last one to encourage you to return to the arena,' said Bion slowly, 'But this is one invitation I think you should accept.'

'Why's that?' challenged Paris. 'Even if the request does come from the Emperor, why should I oblige the man who was responsible for Publius' death?'

'First of all, it's likely that the Emperor has asked for you personally: you know how he supports the myrmillos - and you are the most celebrated myrmillo of the age. And, as Cotilus says, the Plebian Games will be the first big event of his reign. Secondly, I fear that Domitian does not take kindly to being crossed. He's known for executing men over trivialities. He tried to kill his own brother often enough.'

Paris stared at Bion. 'So you think I should do it then?'

'I think you have no choice. We must hope that the Emperor should be satisfied knowing that you came out of retirement just for him.'

Paris gazed out of the window at the sea. 'Much as I hate to leave, we must make haste for Rome. It's now the Ides of October: I have a month to train.'

'What will you do for armour?'

'I've still got my Lion armour and weapons somewhere. I packed it in a chest when we moved here. Cotilus let me keep it - "Just in case you ever come back".'

'He knew you would, the crafty monster,' grinned Bion. 'One last fight, then.'

'One last fight.'

CHAPTER 10

'The myrmillo known as The Lion of the Ludus Magnus, winner of 69 fights, versus the retiarius Eros of the Neronian school in Capua, winner of 23 fights,' Bion read from the programme, as he and Paris waited in the dressing room under the arena. Paris was already in full armour, but for his helmet which was resting on Bion's knees. As usual the Lion's bout was last on the bill that day and they were awaiting a knock on the door that would summon the gladiator to the ring.

'The odds are 50-1 in your favour Paris. People's entire fortunes are riding on you today. He's a complete unknown, this Eros - it's his first fight in Rome.'

'Yes, but he has an impressive number of wins to his name, so I expect him to be an honourable opponent.'

'Still, he doesn't know the ways of the Roman arena. And I'm sure you have a few surprises up your sleeve.'

Paris smiled mysteriously. 'I do have a few novelties planned for my last fight.'

'You'll certainly have the Emperor rooting for you, anyway,' said Bion with an impish smile. The other day he heard a supporter of the Thracians insult the myrmillos and had him thrown to the dogs in the arena.'

There was a sharp rap at the door, and Paris jumped to his feet. He turned to Bion, who raised the helmet over his head. It had always been strictly understood at the amphitheatre that the stagehands who called the Lion would knock, but never enter his dressing room. Bion gasped, therefore, when the door swung open and a portly figure entered the room and closed the door behind him. He was even more surprised when the intruder stepped into the light and he recognised his former master, Diogenes.

The slave hurriedly tried to slip the helmet over Paris' face, but before he could do so, the merchant called out the gladiator's name.

Paris turned to face his old enemy. 'You knew that I was the Lion?'

'I have known for some time. Not everyone subscribes to the gladiator's code of loyalty. And I have always found that enough money buys whatever you want. I think you are acquainted with a gentleman by the name of Iaculator. Rough type, isn't he?'

'It doesn't matter anyway,' said Paris, thoughtfully, placing the helmet over his head. 'This will be my last fight.'

'Really?' said Diogenes, his lips curling in a smile. 'I look forward to it. It may interest you to know that I have sponsored this bout, as my tribute to the new Emperor.'

'So you've resumed your political career, have you, Diogenes?' grinned Bion.

'Why you cheeky little monkey,' retorted Diogenes. 'As it happens, I am standing for aedile here in Rome at the next elections.'

'So, is it true that the Emperor requested my presence?' demanded Paris. 'Did he ask you?'

'Well, not personally,' mumbled Diogenes. 'I've never actually met him. But he had made it known that he would look with great favour on anyone who managed to lure you back to the ring.'

'I suppose it's fitting that you should be sponsoring my last fight: after all I owe my career in the arena to you.'

'You don't need to be polite to me, Paris,' Diogenes sneered. 'I know you hate me for selling you to Corax and for destroying your precious documents. But you did something much worse to me. You stole my son.'

'If he was ever really yours,' said Paris.

Diogenes stared at the ground with a bitter expression. 'Now he is dead,' he snarled and, with both hands, made the gesture to ward of evil spirits.

Paris waited in the darkness behind the heavy bronze doors that opened on to the arena. Though he would not have chosen to fight again, he felt the same emotions as he had always felt before a fight - a feeling of great calm, a sense that the cares of his everyday life were sliding off him like drops of mercury, an impression of invulnerability, as though protected by the cloak of the goddess Fortuna.

A trumpet blast sounded in the arena. Two stagehands pulled back the doors. The mob uttered an hysterical yell as Paris appeared. The rich matrons seated on the podium which ran round the edge of the arena pelted him with yellow flowers. Rulers of different races from all over the Empire, along with their courtiers, also had ringside seats: blond warriors clad in skins from Germania, gorgeously robed Armenians, Nubians with their plumed head-dresses.

As Paris acknowledged the cheers with his curved sword and long shield, he was barely aware of the retiarius, still a small dark figure against the bright glare of the sand.

They approached one another slowly across the arena, the spectators' tension mounting. Paris began to focus on his opponent, assessing the other man's physique, his possible skills or weak points. Most retiarii" were tall, but this one was of exceptional height - and more muscular than most of his fellows. He was dark-skinned - from Egypt or Syria, perhaps.

As they circled one another, gradually drawing closer, there seemed to be something familiar about this man - about his form and his walk. Perhaps they had fought before - in Pompeii or Puteoli. By now, Paris was just twenty yards away from the other gladiator.

Suddenly he felt his limbs go weak. His sword and shield almost slipped from his grasp. The face was now etched with lines of experience, the frame had filled out with powerful muscle, the skin had darkened in the sun of the arena, the torso and legs were covered with wiry black hair, yet there was no doubting it. Eros of Capua, the retiarius, was Lucius, his Lucius, whom he had believed dead. So he survived the disaster at Pompeii, after all. And why was he here now, facing his former lover in the ring?

The answer came to him in a flash. He was certain that Lucius did not suspect his true identity. This was all Diogenes' doing. How perfect, he thought, what a supreme gesture of revenge against them both this was. How carefully Diogenes had planned it. When did he discover that Lucius was alive, Paris wondered? By what stroke of destiny did he learn that I was the Lion?

The other man continued to circle, not a flicker of recognition on his grim features. Of course not, thought Paris, in this golden mask. His body, now with a thick layer of golden hair, had broadened and was marked with scars that Lucius had never known.

As the two men performed the dance of circling and dodges that began any fight between a retiarius and a myrmillo, it occurred to Paris that he should call out to Lucius and identify himself. But would he even hear over the din? And it would almost certainly come as such a shock that Lucius would lose his nerve or even throw down his arms. To wrench off his helmet would have the same effect, or worse.

He needed time to think. But there was no time.

Paris' heart pounded as he made out, through the noise of the rabble, Lucius' voice declaiming the traditional chant of the netman. Although Paris could not hear the words, he knew them by heart: 'I do not seek you but a fish. So why do you run from me, O Gaul?'

With that, the retiarius turned tail and fled, his long limbs skimming the ground, like an athlete on a Greek vase. Paris hesitated for a moment which was reflected in a sudden dip in the racket that filled the amphitheatre. Then he was off in pursuit and the sound rose once more. The retiarius made for one of the narrow ends of the elliptical ring and paused, waiting for his pursuer. Paris stopped some distance away. He recognised the classic manoeuvre: he was pretending to be cornered so as to lure the myrmillo as close as possible. Then he would launch his net.

As he had always done on such situations, Paris dashed forward and the net came whistling towards him. Lucius had aimed a little too high and Paris was able to fling himself forward on the ground and let it fly over him.

Now that the retiarius had lost his net, he could do one of two things: throw the trident or move in for hand-to-hand combat. It was too early in the fight to risk everything and Paris was fully prepared when Lucius came hurtling towards him, uttering a bloodcurdling shriek. Now the audience was really fired up. Paris could see the wealthy enthusiasts of the games hanging over the sides of the ring, howling advice and suggesting possible strokes with violent gestures.

He took the full impact of Lucius' trident on his shield, leaning his body into the blow. He threw it back with an upward motion of the shield and an upper-cut of his sword. As Lucius shifted his grip for a downward plunge of the trident, Paris repulsed it by jamming his sword between the sharpened prongs. For several seconds, the two men were locked together, almost motionless, brute strength against brute strength.

Ben Elliott

Through his eye-holes, Paris looked into Lucius' big dark eyes: they stared back at him like those of a panther on the attack. The musky smell of Lucius' sweating body filtered through Paris' helmet. Paris twisted his sword hard, almost pulling the trident from Lucius' hands. While the retiarius recovered his grip, Paris sprinted a few yards, before turning back to face his adversary. He had stopped right by the tangled net and hurled it behind him, well beyond Lucius' reach.

The other man traced a rapid series of zig-zags, but without approaching any closer. As Paris was sure he would, Lucius hurled the trident. The myrmillo dodged it as he had done so many times in the past. The arena erupted in cheers. He should not have thrown it yet, thought Paris. Too soon, much too soon.

Lucius was poised, tense. He had few options. The net was far beyond his reach. To retrieve the trident, he would have to outrun the other man. And he had already experienced the Lion's speed. Paris knew that this was the moment for the kill and so did his devoted admirers. The chant of 'Cut his throat!' surged around the amphitheatre.

With the speed and curving trajectory of a javelin, Lucius sprinted around Paris towards his trident. Instead of intercepting him, as he so easily could have done, Paris did not budge, turning to follow the other gladiator with his eyes. A roar of disappointment filled the stadium. Lucius picked up his weapon without any loss of speed and, putting some distance between himself and Paris, spun round, the trident poised at shoulder height.

The crowd fell silent. The fight was not following any pattern they recognised. Now the two gladiators, fifty yards apart were staring at each other, motionless. The spectators began to mutter to one another. What had got into the Lion? The fight should be over by now. Why had he missed his chance? Wait and see, the myrmillo's supporters advised their friends. He has another trick up his sleeve as always. The Lion can never be second-guessed.

But for the first time, Paris was not that other being - the Lion: cool, detached, lethal. In the past he had concentrated on one thing only: kill to survive. Now, for the first time in the arena, he was torn by conflicting emotions like any man.

The myrmillo had taken the gladiator's oath before the fight - to die rather than disobey. Yet could he kill this man who had meant so much to him and perhaps still did?

Lucius was prowling towards him, eyes narrowed under his dark brows. He would not throw his trident this time. There would be another hand-to-hand fight, probably to the death. Paris backed slowly away. Shrill voices screamed abuse: 'Has the Lion lost its claws?' 'Is the pussy waiting to be stroked?' These were the spectators who had staked everything on the fight, thought Paris grimly.

From the corner of his eye, he could see the slaves whose task it was to urge on timid fighters. They were gingerly emerging from behind the wooden barriers at the side of the ring which served to protect them and the trainers. Paris could smell the red-hot irons from where he was standing. Cotilus was dancing about next to them, trying to make out what was up: he had long given up attempting to fathom out Paris' unorthodox fighting techniques.

If he did not vanquish Lucius, thought Paris, he would have to face defeat himself. But then how would Lucius feel when he realised that he had killed his former lover unintentionally? Or, worse still, if he removed his helmet for the coup de grace and Lucius had to look into his eyes as he delivered the blow.

No, Paris decided: there was only one possibility. He must win. His reputation in the arena was based on taking risks. Now he must take the greatest risk of his career and win for them both.

Hugging the marble wall, Paris headed at top speed for the centre of the arena. The populace sent up a howl of relief. The Lion had not turned yellow after all. He had been toying with his prey before going in for the kill.

Paris could see the retiarius in hot pursuit. Just as he reached a point in front of the Emperor's box, Paris pulled up short. The crowd gave another roar of approval: the Lion was preparing to slaughter his opponent as a tribute to the new sovereign. Paris was aware of Domitian in his golden diadem and purple cloak craning forward anxiously from his couch. The strange little boy with the abnormally small head, who always accompanied the Emperor to the games, was jumping up and down excitedly beside his master.

Paris leaped forward to engage the retiarius as he sped towards him.

The collision sent a sickening jar through the bodies of both men. The clang of Paris' steel sword-blade against the bronze of Lucius' trident rang through the arena. Darting back, beyond the range of Lucius' weapon, Paris turned his shield sideways, holding his sword inside it, offering it to the retiarius as the bullfighter would his cloak. The shield was polished to a shine and was free of any carving that could have caught the point of a trident. Lucius made repeated thrusts, towards Paris' head, chest and legs, but each time the gladiator threw them off using the shield alone. The retiarius became increasingly desperate, trying every move he knew. The crowd went wild. The netman was beginning to tire.

The trident plunged towards Paris' feet. Lucius' eyes were fixed on its prongs. This time Paris skipped to one side to avoid it.
He launched the shield at Lucius' chest propelled by his full body-weight. Winded, Lucius staggered back, just managing to keep his grip on the trident with his left hand.

Whipping his sword out from behind the shield Paris made a deft swipe across the gladiator's left palm with its tip, forcing the man to drop his weapon. Slipping the shield over his arm, Paris charged Lucius with it once more, sending the man sprawling on the sand of the arena.

Lucius looked up in bemusement, feeling the sharp blade at his throat. Paris stood over him in the pose his admirers knew so well. On this occasion, however, Paris' eyes were fixed, not on the Emperor's box but on the face of his adversary.

'Lucius,' called Paris urgently, attempting to cut through the deafening hubbub of the arena. 'It's Paris.'

'Paris?' murmured the retiarius. 'By Bacchus! You are the Lion?'

'Your father is the sponsor of this fight - did you know that?' continued Paris urgently.

Lucius shook his head blankly.

'He planned this as his revenge on us both. But we will outwit him.'

The crowd were now on their feet. The Lion had always slaked their thirst for blood in the past. Once again, he would not let them down. The chant of 'Cut his throat,' boomed through the auditorium. Paris could see the college of Vestal Virgins in the box next to the Emperor's, waving their thumbs in the sign of death, their shrieks soaring above the others.

The Emperor rose, the white handkerchief in his hand. His eyes swept the arena, then tilted down to the two tiny figures immediately below him. The scrap of white silk fluttered from his hand towards the dirt of the ring.

'Paris, you must deliver the death blow,' Lucius insisted. 'If not, we will both die.'

'Would you have killed me once you realised who I was?'

Lucius glanced away. 'I robbed you of your life once. I could not do it a second time.' He turned his face up to Paris beseechingly: 'Do it quickly. I will not feel it, coming from you. As though you were making love to me one last time.'

Paris shook his head firmly.

The people could not believe their eyes. The Lion was removing his helmet. He tossed back his long blond curls, their gold intensified by the afternoon sunlight and raised his face to the Emperor's box. A gasp went up from those of the crowd who could see him. He was beautiful this great myrmillo - a Ganymede, an Apollo, not disfigured as the rumours said. The word passed round the arena like a swarm of bees. The Lion, our Lion, is a young god.

'Great Caesar,' Paris called out boldly. There was a sudden silence as everyone strained to catch the words of the champion. The spectators' whispered comments were like the sea through shingle. 'As you know I had vowed never to fight again. I returned to the arena one last time as my personal homage to the start of your illustrious reign.' Paris saw the Emperor shift nervously on his couch. The boy with the tiny head was whispering in his ear. 'Every man here can testify to your generosity – for each has received a gift of three hundred sesterces from the imperial coffers.'

Paris paused for the cheers of the crowd to die down. 'I would like to ask a personal boon from the new Emperor. On several occasions, I refused the wooden sword of freedom in the arena. I chose to fight on for the sake of the people of Rome. Now I would ask you, noble Caesar, and the people of Rome, in return for all those occasions when I rejected the gift of freedom, the gift of life, to grant freedom and mercy to this opponent of mine. You who favour the myrmillos, allow me to show that while we may fight like beasts we can also be merciful, like men.'

The spectators shifted uneasily in their seats, muttering to one another, wondering how the Emperor would react. He was engaged in an intense conversation with the little boy, who was nodding furiously and gesturing with his short skinny arms. At last, Domitian rose from his couch. Paris had never known such silence in the packed amphitheatre.

'People of Rome,' he proclaimed, in a thin, nervous tone. 'You have heard this man's request. Shall a myrmillo show his opponent mercy? You must decide.'

The crowd shot to its feet, fists raised high in the gesture that signified clemency for a fallen gladiator. How could they refuse the request of their young god?

The small-headed boy was jumping up and down with delight on the Emperor's couch, holding onto his master's toga. The Emperor smiled and nodded his head to the myrmillo. Paris acknowledged the favour he had been granted with a low bow to the Emperor, before turning to the rest of the amphitheatre and raising his sword in salute.

Paris insisted that Lucius should accompany him to the Imperial box for the presentation of the prize money.

Domitian bore a superficial family resemblance to his brother, but without any of Titus' confidence or charm. His elaborate gold diadem only partly concealed his baldness. He blushed when he spoke. 'I hope you realise how much you owe this man,' said the Emperor to the retiarius.

Lucius smiled. 'Even you, Caesar, cannot imagine how much.'

Domitian descended the steps of his throne to present Paris with the prize money. 'You have done me a great service, my Lion of the arena,' he told Paris, keeping his voice low so that his courtiers could not hear. 'The people of Rome will not easily forget this day and a share of the glory will fall on me. My brother Titus was a very popular ruler. It is not easy for me to follow him. I know what they say about me: that I spend all my time locked in my room catching flies. But, after today, they will remember that Domitian granted their wishes in the amphitheatre.'

He put his arm round the small-headed boy. 'People think that because his head is so small, his brain is tiny, too, but he is wiser than most men. I wanted to grant your request for mercy myself, but it was he who advised me to let the people decide.

'He knew that the multitude would be of the same mind and they would love me far more if I left it up to them. But he also told me that there is a story behind this request. If so, I'd like to hear it.'

Paris and Lucius looked at one another and smiled. Paris turned back to the Emperor with a nod.

The Emperor led the two men into the private chamber, where Paris had revealed his identity to Titus. The little boy scampered behind on short spindly legs. Paris and Lucius explained how they had been friends years ago at Diogenes' villa in Pompeii. Blushing, Lucius explained that he had hidden Paris' documents and recounted how Diogenes destroyed them.

When they reached this point in the tale, Domitian frowned: 'I know this Diogenes. Was he not the sponsor of today's games? Tampering with an imperial decree is a serious crime. I hear the man is anxious to dine with me. Well, he shall have his wish.'

The Emperor turned a solemn face to Paris: 'In recompense for the wrong that has been done to you and in recognition of the glory you have earned for me today, I pledge that, as long as I am Emperor, neither of you shall be required to appear in the arena again. In token of this promise, you will both receive the ivory ticket of freedom.'

Lucius travelled back with Paris and Bion to the villa on the coast. Since the retiarius had renounced his name and position as the son of a wealthy merchant, he had lived a nomadic existence, lodging in gladiator schools and taverns, so it did not take him long to gather his few possessions.

The three men spent long hours sitting in the bay window of the dining room, enjoying the last of the autumn sunshine and listening to the pounding of the waves. There was much to tell. Paris described how he had decided to adopt the identity of the Lion in the Roman arena. He did not need to say more. Lucius - as any gladiator in the Empire - knew as much about the Lion's achievements as Paris himself. Bion gave his account of how he and his master had followed the counsel of Isis which had saved their lives.

Most of all, Paris and Bion were anxious to hear Lucius' story. How had he escaped the destruction of Pompeii, where so many gladiators had perished? And how had Diogenes tracked him down and hired him for the match with Paris?

Pacing nervously round the curve of pillars, as he recalled the horror of the calamity, Lucius recalled the severe earthquakes of the days leading up to the eruption of Mount Vesuvius. 'People were pouring out of the city on foot and in carts. It was obvious to anyone who had witnessed the disaster of Nero's reign, that the only hope was to evacuate the city - though no one realised how much worse this would be. I pleaded with Corax to leave with the gladiators but he feared that they would seize the chance to escape and his livelihood would be lost. He had convinced himself that the danger would pass. He told me, however, that as a free man, I was at liberty to flee.

'I decided to offer my services to the Neronian school at Capua. The roads from the city were choked with citizens fleeing on foot. Many were wheeling carts, loaded with possessions. As I was on horseback, I was able to avoid the crush. I was still some distance from Capua when the volcano blew. A pillar of fire towered into the heavens and blotted out the sky. A black cloud, like wall of lead, moved across the face of the earth, enveloping everything and everyone. Suddenly I found myself in pitch darkness and was forced to dismount and wait. I was certain that the world had come to an end. It seemed that we had been transported, while still alive, to the underworld.

'For a long time it was impossible to tell whether it was day or night, then, gradually, I began to see again: first my own limbs, then the ground, and still later nearby trees. Finally, in a kind of permanent twilight, I was able to resume my journey.

'Once in Capua, I decided to take the name of Eros and break all links with the past. That way I could start a new life. I knew that everyone would assume that I was dead. I thought that perhaps that would be a blessing for you, Paris. It was certainly better for my father to think of me that way, even though I was not sure if he had survived the disaster.

'Having won many victories and built up a considerable fortune in Capua, I was invited to fight in Rome by a scout recruiting for the school founded by the new Emperor. My father must have spotted me while I was training in the capital. But until today, I was not sure if he still lived.'

Bion, who had been leaning against Paris' legs, knelt up excitedly.

'Or, maybe he furnished the scout with your likeness and sent him to seek you out in all the schools of the country,' he suggested.

'That's possible,' replied Lucius. 'I think he would go to any lengths to avenge himself.'

Between these discussions, Paris and Lucius took long walks together on the beach. Winter was setting in and, although some days were bathed in the gold light of a low sun, others were grey and stormy.

'I thought about you so often in these years,' Lucius sighed. 'I wondered what had become of you and thought it strange that, after your success in Pompeii, you had not made a name for yourself in Rome. How wrong I was!'

Though almost everything in their lives had changed, the two men realised that their bond had survived and deepened.

'In the years since we were separated, I have never loved anyone else,' Lucius admitted. 'Everyone I met, I compared with you.'

'I believed that I hated you,' Paris confessed. 'But in time I understood that I had acted with the stubbornness of youth. Beneath the anger and bitterness, I still loved you.'

One evening at supper, Bion was agog with the latest gossip from Rome. Domitian had invited Diogenes to dine with him, just as he had promised. The sycophantic merchant had eagerly accepted and had arrived at the palace laden with gifts which the Emperor had received most graciously. The banquet had proceeded cordially until Domitian pulled one of the surprise attacks for which he was famous. Out of the blue, he had challenged Diogenes over the destruction of Paris' documents.

Threatened with exile and the confiscation of all of his wealth, Diogenes broke down and confessed to the crime. The Emperor duly announced that he would only confiscate half of the merchant's goods, which would be given to his son as his rightful inheritance, and that the wretched man would be exiled anyway - to a small island off the coast of Sicilia, where he was now ensconced.

'He should find it easy enough to be elected aedile there, at least,' remarked Bion innocently and the three men laughed.

In spring, the temple to the memory of Publius, that Paris had ordered to be built on a headland near the villa, was finally completed. Priestesses of the goddess Fortuna came from her shrine at Praeneste to perform the ceremony of dedication. Bion had spent weeks on the preparations and a lavish banquet awaited the guests in the dining room overlooking the shore. It would be accompanied by a chorus of singers newly arrived from Alexandria.

As the lovers offered incense to the gods, Paris admired the statue of Publius. It was lifesize and the artist had captured an amazing likeness. Paris, the Lion of the arena, would never forget the Praetorian Guard and all he had learned from him. The statue of Lucius, which had caused him so much concern, had not been required. As the incense billowed up into the cloudless sky, mingling with the tang of wild thyme and rosemary, Paris reached into the folds of Lucius' toga and took hold of his lover's powerful hand. He needed no images. He had the flesh-and-blood Lucius by his side.

The goddess had smiled on them once more.